THE COMPLETE COLLECTION

TALES FROM THE HOTEL BENTMOORE

SHELBY CROSS

This is a work of fiction. Names, characters, places and incidents are products of the author's imagination or are used fictitiously and are not to be construed as real. Any resemblance to actual events, locales, organizations or persons, living or dead, is entirely coincidental.

Visit http://shelbycrosswriter.blogspot.com for updates, news, and more.

Cover and Interior: Streetlight Graphics

Dedicated to my Husband

Table of Contents

Alice . . . . *.5*

Deborah *36*

Mark and Audra *84*

Elizabeth *121*

Alice

ALICE BARR WAS THE model high-powered business woman you might see walking down a busy New York street: sophisticated, well dressed, and in a great hurry to be somewhere else. She was an executive working in a well known Wall Street company, and her salary reflected her station. Respected for her job title as well as her generosity and philanthropic work, she drifted within the circles of high society, the creme of New York's crop.

She was a modern woman, opinionated, sure of herself. But she had one dark secret, one that would mortify her if it ever got out: Alice needed to be disciplined. She craved the strong hand of a dominant male on her soft derriere, and when she went too long without it, her mood would eventually deteriorate, her temper becoming alarmingly short, and her patience disappearing completely. It was like she became a different woman.

She needed to be controlled, tamed and broken like a wild and exotic animal. But she could not allow just anyone to treat her in such a way; she could not let her secret get out. She was too afraid it would stain her reputation, make her a figure of derision.

And so, she became a frequent visitor to the Hotel Bentmoore.

On this particular trip to the Hotel Bentmoore, Alice had made arrangements for a short visit, just a two night stay, to celebrate landing an account that could shoot her career into the highest stratosphere of her company, maybe even make her a board member. It was what she had been striving for, a culmination of years of hard work, and she couldn't imagine a better place to celebrate.

It wasn't long before her liaison, Mr. Brooks, was knocking on the door to her suite. No matter for many days Alice had scheduled her stay at the hotel, she always tried to get the suite: it was roomier, had a large hot tub, and the windows had a wonderful view of the mountains beyond. And if she could afford it, why should she not have the best?

"Yes?"

"Mr. Sinclaire welcomes you back, ma'am, and would like to confirm ten o'clock tonight."

"Tell Mr. Sinclaire thank you, and ten o'clock is fine."

"Thank you, ma'am."

Mr. Brooks quickly left by the elevator, and Alice shut the door. Mr. Brooks had been the acting liaison between her and Mr. Sinclaire for a long time now, yet Alice still felt the thrill every time Mr. Brooks would seek her out to confirm her scheduled activity with her host.

Alice ate her meal in the hotel dining room, comfortable in her own company, and took her time enjoying the food. Then, she returned to her suite, and carefully prepared for the night ahead, redoing her hair and donning the outfit she had brought with her for just this occasion.

At ten o'clock, Mr. Brooks returned.

"I need another few minutes," Alice called out from behind the door.

"Very well, ma'am," Mr. Brooks answered back.

Alice waited just inside the door, not going very far. In fact, she did nothing but watch the clock, fidgeting for a good ten minutes. When she decided it had been long enough, she opened the door, saw her liaison waiting just outside, and walked through.

Mr. Brooks made no mention of her tardiness; it was not up to him to care one way or the other if she was late for her activity. He also did not notice her attire, or at least, pretended not to. Her outfit was hardly something she would wear on the streets of New York, or anywhere else in public, for that matter. But Mr. Brooks simply walked ahead. Alice fell a good few steps behind.

"This way, ma'am," he said, keeping his voice, and his expression, completely neutral. Alice followed dutifully, but silently, making no noise, not even from her high stiletto heels. The carpet muffled the sounds of her footsteps.

Soon, Mr. Brooks had led her down the elevator and across the hallway that brought her to the activity room. He opened the door and gestured her through. Alice gave her liaison a small smile, then walked on, and had the satisfaction of hearing Mr. Brooks lock the door behind her.

The room was quite familiar to her now, but she looked around anyway, searching for signs of any changes, and smiled when she saw none. She liked to have the same room, in the same layout; the familiarity was comforting.

The room was rather large, with pale lavender walls and a marble floor, polished to a high shine. In the far corner was the bed, a large four-poster with silk sheets that matched the walls, looking luxurious and magnificent. It was flanked by two single-drawer side tables, containing a variety of smaller sex toys.

A high wooden saddle chair sat off to the side of the room, well padded and screwed into the floor. Next to it was the only other piece of furniture in the room: a wide, double-doored mahogany wardrobe, dark and elegant. Alice knew for a fact that the wardrobe did not contain any clothes, save for a robe or two.

The room itself would probably not raise any particular suspicions to the average passerby, unless one took a good look around, and began to notice all the heavy metal hooks bolted into the walls, floor, and ceiling. One devilish hook even poked out from the door behind her.

Mr. Sinclaire was waiting for her, as usual. He was by the bed, facing the door, leaning his shoulder against the wall. He wore a short black robe, belted at the waist, showing the wispy blond hairs that matted his broad chest. Alice's eyes grazed his long, muscular legs, clean lines, and slightly tanned skin. The hairs on his legs were a shade lighter than the rest of him, bleached from hours spent outside wearing shorts, and they looked whisper soft.

Alice knew his hands were large, and his fingers long and knuckled; but right now, she couldn't see them. Mr. Sinclaire's arms were crossed: he looked peeved.

"You're late again," he said sternly.

"I'm sorry, Sir. I didn't mean to be." She tried to hide the smile tugging at her lips. He hated it when she arrived late, which was precisely why she did so.

"Alice, what am I to do with you? You try my patience," he sighed, straightening up from the wall. "Come here."

Alice dutifully obeyed, walking straight and erect toward her host, looking at him innocently. He stopped her a few feet away.

"And what exactly are you wearing this evening?" His brows furrowed.

"Do you like it? It fits me well, don't you think?"

She had donned a crisply ironed white shirt, collared and short sleeved. But it was buttoned up only until the rise of her breasts, leaving the swells of her cleavage quite prominent. The shirt was short, ending barely at the waist; if she raised her arms at all, the narrow curve of her midriff would immediately be exposed. Her skirt, navy blue and pleated, might have been part of a school girl's uniform, except that it was also indecently short, falling just below the pert swells of her ass. The high heeled stiletto shoes and thin, matching blue tie around her neck completed the ensemble. She looked like a saucy, impertinent school girl.

"How it fits you is irrelevant. That outfit is hardly something a woman of your stature should be wearing," Mr. Sinclaire said. His eyes were smoldering under his heavy blond brows. Alice didn't know if it was anger or lust, but at the moment, she didn't much care: either one would satisfy her.

"I'm afraid your choice of outfit, along with your tardiness, requires a swift punishment. Up against the chair, please."

Alice eyed the saddle chair and paused. She was feeling very insolent tonight. Of course, Mr. Sinclaire noticed right away. He shook his head and sighed again.

"Ahh, Alice, I see you are going to be very naughty tonight....Well. I'll be breaking you of that first thing. Now, are you going to lean up against the chair on your own like a good girl, or will I have to help you?"

Alice didn't answer, but looked at him impudently.

Mr. Sinclaire's expression became serious as he walked over to the wardrobe. When he turned around again, he was holding two soft leather wrist cuffs, one in each hand, connected by a long thick chain. He walked towards Alice in long strides, holding the cuffs in front of him.

Alice bolted across the room. Mr. Sinclaire came after her, maneuvering her until she was cornered against the wall by the bed. He quickly caught her around the waist and wrestled her face down onto the bed, holding her in place with his long body, and pulled her arms out from under her. Alice bucked her hips and tried to lift him off her; he pushed her into the mattress harder, using his body weight to keep her still.

She continued to struggle, but Mr. Sinclaire quickly had one leather strap buckled around one thin wrist; and then, pinning her arms together above her head, he buckled the other wrist, too. Alice's arms were now linked together, leaving only a small space of chain to separate them.

Pulling her hard by the waist, Mr. Sinclaire stood Alice up.

Immediately, she tried to run again, but her host nonchalantly grabbed the chain between her wrists and pulled, and she was jerked against his chest. Looking into her eyes, taking in her defiant expression, Mr. Sinclaire began to wind the chain in his hand. It was somewhat heavy, but he did it with practiced ease.

Now, pulling her struggling form by the chain, he dragged her over to the saddle chair, stepped around it, and unceremoniously pulled her over it.

Alice grunted from the impact of the padding against her stomach; the chair was rather tall, and hit her just below the ribs. But Mr. Sinclaire pulled her over the chair even further, so that she was bent straight down the middle, and her feet could barely touch the floor.

He continued to pull her hands down until he got a grunt from the stretched woman, then unwound the chain from his hand and looped it through the hook set into the floor for just this purpose. Alice was now trussed up against the chair, her ass in the air, and not going anywhere.

She struggled against the chain for a minute, twisting her body, trying to pull up; but it was no use. She had known, of course, that it would be no use. But she still had to try, every time.

Now Mr. Sinclaire stepped behind her, taking his time. He looked over her bent form, still struggling against the chain, wiggling becomingly; her long, well shaped legs, dangling over the chair, straight and smooth; the jutting mounds of her presenting ass, the crescent shapes peaking out from her short skirt.

With her butt raised as it was, the indecent skirt had lifted from her struggles, and was now showing off the curving bottom swells of her ass delightfully. Mr. Sinclaire had a good view of the white translucent panties she wore underneath: they barely concealed the shadowy crack dividing her twin cheeks, and, below that, the smooth, bulging mound of her pussy. He took note of the wet stain spreading in the crotch of her panties, making them stick to her smooth skin. From the chase and their struggle, Alice was already obviously turned on.

"You have been very naughty tonight, Alice," Mr. Sinclaire said. "I'm afraid I'll have to start you off with ten of my best--with the crop." Alice gasped. "Yes, ten with the crop, and we'll just have to see how your mood is after *that*." Alice fought the chain even more; Mr. Sinclaire waited for her to calm down, smiling ominously. Alice couldn't see him smiling, of course. She was stuck looking down at the floor.

When she was done with her struggles and breathing heavily, he walked over to the wardrobe and returned with a long, thin riding crop. He took his place behind her.

"We'll have to rid you of this skirt, of course," he said nonchalantly. "You shouldn't be wearing it anyway. But then, you knew that--saucy girl." Alice could almost hear the chuckle in his voice, and she smiled; but she shook her head no.

"No?" He said in mock surprise. "I will have to do a better job of teaching you what I expect. 'No' is not the answer I'm looking for."

He reached out and gently put his wide hands on her pale thighs, squeezing lightly; Alice inhaled with a hiss through her teeth. He began to trail his hands up over her slope of her butt, and as he did, he took the skirt with him, until the indecent and naughty piece of material rested across Alice's waist. Her pantied ass was completely on view for him now, thrusting out invitingly, just begging to be abused. He took a moment to admire her smooth cheeks, and the light creases sloping under each crescent moon, like the smiling mouth of a satisfied feline.

Hooking two fingers into the hem of her panties, he slowly pulled them down her hips, exposing her rear crack and more smooth pale skin, until they stretched across her thighs. Now he could see the barest glimpse of her pussy lips from between her legs, coral pink and slightly moist. He wanted to touch her, trail a finger up and down her soft pussy lips, slip a finger or two inside. But he held himself back.

Taking the riding crop in hand, he moved to the side of the chair. She would kick, he knew; and he didn't feel like getting hit by her shoes.

"Are you ready to learn your lesson, Alice?"

Alice shook her head stubbornly.

"No? Well, too bad." With a gleam in his eyes, he raised the crop high into the air, then swung it down with a hiss...landing it directly on Alice's soft, upthrust rump.

SMACK!

Alice arched her back up and pulled on the chain, howling loudly.

SMACK! SMACK! SMACK!

Mr. Sinclaire struck hard and fast, not giving her any time to recover between blows. It stung like hell, and she kicked up her heels wildly, trying to escape the awful stinging.

SMACK SMACK SMACK--

Alice was shrieking now, trying to get her host to stop; but he paid her no mind, and kept going.

SMACK SMACK SMACK--

By now, Alice was crying a little, and pulling desperately on the chain. But it would do no use; it never did. She rested her head against the chair and waited for the final blow, the end of her promised and deserved punishment.

Mr. Sinclaire waited. He gazed at her blushing butt, the angry red welts that now criss-crossed her soft pliant skin, and watched as she clenched her bottom anxiously. He had promised ten, and there was still one more to go; he knew Alice had counted in her head just as he had. But he waited until Alice had calmed down a bit. At last, she unclenched her butt cheeks and relaxed her thighs.

Just as Alice took a shuddering, calming breath, he struck.

SMACK!

Alice screamed furiously. She writhed her whole body for a moment, then went limp.

Mr. Sinclaire watched her, letting his eyes graze now and then across the thin red lines burning across her ass. Then he put the crop down on one of the side tables and unhooked the chain binding her to the floor.

"You may get up now, Alice. But I think we will keep the cuffs on you for the rest of the evening--a re-

minder of what will happen if you disobey me again."
He looked her over. "And now I think we can move on
with this evening's activity. Take off your clothes."

With shaking hands, Alice straightened herself
up and pushed the hair out of her face, looking at him
insolently.

"Strip, miss," Mr. Sinclaire ordered sternly. Alice
pouted, but dutifully began to take off her clothes. Her
host removed the chain from between her cuffs just long
enough for her to pull off her shirt, and then he hooked
it back in once more. Alice could separate her hands to a
distance about three feet wide, but that was it--and that
was how she would stay for the rest of the night.

When Alice was done taking off all her clothes, she
turned to face him defiantly, pushing her hair back and
looking slightly devious. Mr. Sinclaire took notice of
her attitude and grunted. She was feeling quite cheeky
tonight; but he could handle that. He would break her
of her will before he let her leave this room. But first he
wanted to look at her naked body.

"Under the light," he ordered, pointing. Alice moved
to stand directly under the chandelier illuminating the
middle of the room, which also happened to be right
above another hook set into the floor. She stood proudly,
her arms to her sides, giving him a knowing look.

Alice had a tiny waist, one of the smallest he'd ever
seen. Below that, her hips widened in delicious curves,

narrowing again slightly at her soft, creamy thighs. Alice had a definite hourglass figure, smooth and supple, one that any woman would be proud to have.

But what really stood out from her form were Alice's large breasts, round, perfectly shaped, and deliciously soft. Mr. Sinclaire knew from first hand experience that they were completely natural, not the result of any surgery or implants, despite their size and perfect upthrust shape.

Her aureoles were a rosy pink, crinkled and wide; and centered perfectly inside each one were her dark, crowning nipples. Right now, they lay flat against her aureoles; but Mr. Sinclaire knew that given enough enticement, they would peak out wantonly from her breasts, begging to be touched.

"Kneel," he growled. Alice lowered to her knees but kept her back stiff and proud. She kept her hands locked together in front of her, and her chain rattled on the floor.

Mr. Sinclaire stepped in front of her and grabbed the chain roughly, looping it twice inside the hook below, effectively chaining her to the floor under the light. She could try to remove the chain from the hook, of course. She had done it before. That punishment had been rather severe: she hadn't been able to sit for two days.

Mr. Sinclaire pulled off his robe, revealing his massive prick. It was not fully erect yet to the point that it touched the skin of his belly, but it stood out boldly in front of him, swaying a bit as he moved. He stepped up to Alice's kneeling form and stood in front of her, his twitching cock mere inches from her mouth.

"Take it in your mouth. Now!"

For a moment, Alice's eyes met his, and he wondered if she would refuse. But then, she tilted her mouth to his cock, opened her lips invitingly, and pulled his long length inside. Mr. Sinclaire shuddered in pleasure and tilted his head back.

Alice lowered her face down his cock as far as she could, feeling his warm pulsing prick fill her mouth and slide down her throat. Mr. Sinclaire had a wonderful cock, one Alice found fascinating, and incredibly erotic. Just looking at it made her pelvis tighten; holding it in her mouth, sucking on it gently and feeling the skin pull across her tongue, made her sigh in delight.

The vibration from her sigh jolted up Mr. Sinclaire's cock, and he sucked in his breath. He was fully erect now inside her mouth, and her lips were stretched wide around his cock.

Inspired by his reaction to her sigh, Alice hummed against the meat filling her mouth; Mr. Sinclaire groaned and pulled out--the sensation was just too tantalizing. If he stayed in her mouth, he would lose control too quickly. With Alice, that would simply not do.

But Alice lunged for his cock with her open mouth, trapping it between her lips and sucking mightily, creating a vacuum between his cock and her warm, stubborn lips. Mr. Sinclaire grabbed her by the shoulders and pushed himself back. She was certainly going to keep him on his toes tonight; he smiled at the challenge, then made his face look stern.

"You have a lot of energy tonight; let's release some of it," he said. He walked over to one of the side tables and came back with a large, vibrating dildo. He held it out to her.

"Play with yourself. Make yourself come--it will relax you a bit so we can continue with tonight's activities at a more leisurely pace." Alice looked at the dildo but made no move to take it. "Do it, Alice," he growled. Alice shook her head no.

With a bellow of anger, Mr. Sinclaire quickly unhooked the chain from the floor, yanked her up, and dragged Alice back to the saddle chair. This time he looped the chain into the hook tight enough that her arms stretched taunt to the floor and her butt stuck up straight in the air; her feet couldn't touch the floor at all. He knew she would feel completely helpless like this, unable to struggle even a bit, and smiled thinly. He took off her shoes.

"If you won't release your energy one way, I'll release it for you another," he whispered, and returned with the riding crop.

Now Alice felt the first stirrings of true nervousness. When Mr. Sinclaire did not tell her how many she could expect with the crop, it meant only one thing: he would keep going until she was beaten down and broken completely. It excited her, but scared her at the same time. And with her butt as high as it was, her soft pussy lips were exposed between her legs, vulnerable to the bite of the crop.

Mr. Sinclaire took his stance by her side and began to beat her ass.

SMACK SMACK SMACK SMACK--

She kicked up her heels and tried to arch her back; she pulled at the chain; she wiggled as much as she could. It did no good. Mr. Sinclaire kept smacking her ass her with quick, steady strokes, never altering his rhythm or speed, and wearing a look of grim determination on his face. The crop came down again, and again, and again, until Alice had lost count as well as all sense of her composure.

SMACK SMACK SMACK--

After some time, Alice began to yell, and then scream, and then sob; the beating was one of the worst he had given her in a long time. But he kept going, swinging the crop up and smacking it against her ass, until Alice was begging for mercy, crying uncontrollably. The pain from her butt was like fire, a scalding, burning flame, scorching lines like a branding iron across her vulnerable skin. But Mr. Sinclaire did not stop, and the spanking seemed to go on forever.

Finally, when Alice's cries had turned into a long, plaintive keening, Mr. Sinclaire lowered the crop in his hand.

"Are you ready to finally obey now?" He asked her softly.

"Yes, Sir," she hiccuped, all resistance broken. Mr. Sinclaire unhooked her chain. Using it as a leash, he lead her to the bed, her arms out in front of her; then he crawled on, dragging her with him. He kept pulling until they were kneeling across from each other in the center of the bed; then, reaching over, he grabbed the dildo, turned it on, and handed it to her.

"Between your legs now," he said.

Alice took the vibrator from his hand. She looked at for a minute, taking in the smooth tubular silicone, the angled tip, the way it hummed away in her palm, making her whole arm vibrate. She turned it in her hand so that it was facing towards her, and lowered it between her legs.

With her other hand, she reached down and opened her pussy lips, spreading her knees a bit as she did. Then, she gently brought the vibrating toy to her crotch, settling it right on her clitoris. Alice sucked in her breath and closed her eyes.

At first, Alice didn't move the dildo, but simply pressed it against her throbbing clit. But soon, she began to slowly rub it up and down her slick inner folds, oiling the thick rod with the cunt juices that drenched her pussy, all the way down her inner thighs. The dildo glistened as it moved with increasing speed, sliding up and down between her splayed legs.

When Mr. Sinclaire took note of the twitches fluttering across her thighs, the tightening of her eyelids, and the slight tension around her face, he gently pulled her hand, and the dildo, away from her cunt. Alice's eyes opened in confusion.

"Take my dick in your mouth," he ordered.

With one hand, Alice took Mr. Sinclaire's long cock, and lowered her mouth to it. Holding his prick by the thick shaft at the base of his balls, she licked and sucked, gliding her warm wet mouth up and down his enormous prick, working him over until Mr. Sinclaire grunted and pulled out.

"Now use the dildo again," he growled.

She timidly obeyed, stuffing the vibrating toy inside her swollen slit, moaning from the delicious sensation the dildo was eliciting from her sensitive clit. She moved it in a circular motion this time, rubbing it in tight rings between her labia, making tiny "oh" sounds every time it touched her pulsing center. But when she began to move in a faster rhythm, her host stopped her again.

"My turn," he said, pulling away the dildo.

She gobbled him up in her mouth, sucking hungrily, pulling him all the way down her tongue. She kept pulling him in until her lips were grazing against the soft down of his pubic hair, and he could feel the back of her throat. He groaned loudly and thrust, twice, three times, lost in the heady thrill of having his entire length slip down her hot mouth, all the way down her dilated slender neck. When his balls began to tighten up in a familiar feeling, he stopped and pulled away.

"The dildo now."

Alice whimpered. Mr. Sinclaire helped her bring the toy back to her pussy, drenched by now and glistening with her cunt juices. He helped her stuff the dildo back inside her soft lips, placing his hand over hers and rubbing until she began to move on her own; and then he watched as she played with herself, moving the toy up, down, and around, undulating her body in complete abandon, trying to bring herself off. But he kept stopping her before she could.

In this way, Mr. Sinclaire had them take turns, Alice working both her host and herself, until they were both on the brink of orgasm...the slightest touch might send either one of them over the edge. When Mr. Sinclaire knew the time had come, he brought Alice's hand up to her crotch, and pressed her head down so that the tip of his cock touched her bottom lip.

"Take me in your mouth and rub the vibrator across your cunt at the same time."

Obediently, Alice did as she was told, swallowing him up as much as she could and sucking desperately, while at the same time rubbing the vibrator gently across her tingling, swollen pussy. She began to moan from pleasure; and each moan made her mouth vibrate around Mr. Sinclaire's cock, bringing him to new heights of ecstasy. He thrusted into her mouth again, pounding his prick down her throat aggressively, using it like a stretched open cunt and getting a series of plaintive moans from the impassioned woman.

Alice was rushing over the edge, jerking the humming vibrator across her cunt in a wild frenzy, groaning loudly around Mr. Sinclaire's cock. Right before she came, she cried out, but it was muffled around her host's swollen prick. The orgasm rose and exploded, and she cried out again, clamping her lips around his member and holding him in a vise-like grip.

Mr. Sinclaire grabbed onto the back of her head and thrust his member deeper down her throat, enjoying the exquisite thrills of her moans vibrating around his prick. As he deep-throated her, her low moans rose in pitch and intensity until she was screaming around his cock, lost in her own orgasm, and he went over the edge himself, exploding in her mouth, shooting his sticky cum down her throat and forcing her to swallow hard.

And Alice swallowed it all, sucking as she came, bucking her hips against the humming dildo between her legs and choking out muffled cries around Mr. Sinclaire's prick, as the waves of her own orgasm still washed over her.

Finally, when the cum stopped shooting out of Mr. Sinclaire's prick with such force, he pulled out his softening member from her face with a wet plop. Alice was breathing hard, taking deep rasping breaths in and out of her glistening mouth, and she fell onto the bed, closing her eyes. Mr. Sinclaire joined her, making the bed shake under the force of his collapse.

They lay across the bed together, Mr. Sinclaire putting a possessive arm across her waist. Their breaths slowed, and Alice rolled to her side and snuggled into the crook of his arm. She wouldn't be sleeping on her back tonight; her butt hurt like hell. She smiled.

"How do you feel?" Mr. Sinclaire asked her.

"Good," she said languidly.

"Got some of the that energy out of you?"

"Yes."

He looked at her shrewdly. "But not all of it."

He looked for the vibrator, and reached for it across the bed. Alice watched him in surprise, then made a sound of protest. Her host shushed her quickly.

"Now, now, no objections. It won't do any good--unless you want more of the crop?" Alice shut her mouth.

Mr. Sinclaire had her come two more times that night, using the vibrator alone. He had her suck his cock again, too, and gobble it up inside her hot humming mouth until he shot his cum down her throat for a second time.

And so, by the time Mr. Sinclaire finally decided she could go, Alice barely had the stamina to walk. In fact, he had to help her dress, holding her clothes while she slipped her limbs through them, a task he didn't seem to mind. She was a different woman now from the one who had walked into the room--shy, demure...she passed him timid glances as she put on her shoes.

"Put some cream on your ass when you get back to your room, Alice," Mr. Sinclaire advised her as they waited for Mr. Brook's return. "Otherwise tomorrow will be hell. Those welts will not stop me from punishing you again if I need to." At that moment Mr. Brooks arrived, opening the door and sweeping his arm wide for her to pass.

For a second, a mischievous gleam came to Alice's eyes, and a bit of her former sauciness returned.

"I would hope not, Sir," she answered, and had the satisfaction of hearing Mr. Sinclaire chuckle as she walked out the door.

*****

The next day Alice woke up late and lazy, stretching her limbs and rising slowly. She rubbed her butt: some light hiking had been planned for the day, but maybe that wasn't such a good idea. Alice decided some quality time in the hot tub was in order.

She ate lunch in her suite, then went down to the hotel spa and had a long massage. By the time Mr. Brooks came to collect her that night, she felt like a different woman from the one who had entered the hotel yesterday: rested, almost languid.

But not to the point of meekness, oh no; she was ready to show Mr. Sinclaire their activities of the night before had not tamed her, not in the least.

But she didn't arrive late, and she didn't put on the schoolgirl outfit again. She wasn't feeling *that* brazen.

When Mr. Sinclaire saw her walk in the door of their activity room at the agreed upon time, she was wearing a long, slinky yellow gown, tight and sleeveless. Adorning her feet were strap sandal shoes. Her host nodded in approval.

"Much better," he said. "You look beautiful."

"Thank you." She cast her eyes down. Much of the fight had been taken out of her yesterday, but Mr. Sinclaire knew her moment of complacency would soon pass, and he would have to be ready. He smiled in anticipation.

"Did you put some cream on your ass, like I told you to?"

"Yes, Sir."

"Let me see. Go to the chair--lean over and lift your dress."

There eyes did battle for a moment, but then Alice yielded and she walked over to the saddle chair. She began to lift her dress, but made a show of it for him, circling her hips and shifting her feet, so that Mr. Sinclaire got a view of her skin inch by inch. He allowed her some fun, giving him a peep show, enjoying the presentation of her long, womanly legs and well contoured thighs. But when she got to the gently sloping curve of her butt, she stopped. He frowned.

"Keep going, Alice."

She turned her head and gave him an impish look. Mr. Sinclaire strode over, pushed her forward, and yanked the dress up past her waist.

She was not wearing any panties underneath. Her ass was bare, smooth, and completely exposed to his view. She arched it back and wiggled it at him provocatively.

"It amazes me sometimes how fast you heal," he murmured, drinking in the delicious sight of her naked bottom. Alice wiggled some more. She couldn't see her host smiling behind her.

"Take off your dress."

With slow, graceful movements, Alice complied. On past visits, she had made him rip her clothes off--but that was not planned for tonight. And anyway, she liked the dress.

By the time she was naked, Mr. Sinclaire had disrobed as well, so that that they stood facing each other in all their glory, and Alice gave him a look that said very clearly: *let the games begin.*

He took her hand to lead her to the bed; she pulled her hand back; he grabbed her by the wrist and dragged her. She struggled, pulling her weight away.

When he got to the edge of the bed, he sat down and pulled her across his lap, holding her down so that her face was pressed into the mattress. He clamped her legs down with one of his own, and without further ado, began to spank her across his lap, hard.

SLAP SLAP SLAP SLAP--

He spanked her with his open hand, watching her butt wobble and clench from the blows. She didn't cry out, but grabbed the sheet with white-knuckled fingers, squeezing tightly. Occasionally she tried to rise up, but Mr. Sinclaire's hand in the small of her back kept her down in position quite effectively.

After the beating he had given her the night before, Mr. Sinclaire reasoned this spanking must hurt even more; but Alice gave no sign of it, and kept quiet. Mr. Sinclaire, meanwhile, was enjoying himself immensely, his cock already thick and hard under Alice's wiggling hips.

When a crimson blush began to shine across her ass and Alice started giving out a short yelp after each blow, he stopped.

"Apologize for your impudence."

"I'm sorry, Sir."

Mr. Sinclaire smiled. "Now lick me."

Alice reached over, poked out her tongue, and licked his hip. Mr. Sinclaire slapped her ass again.

"You know what I meant, Alice. Lick my dick."

Grinning playfully, Alice dutifully slid her head down his lap and licked her host's long prick with her soft, velvety tongue. Like a sleek cat, she lapped at his member until he was wet and glistening. Mr. Sinclaire watched her bent head, taking note of her confidence, the way she spread her legs across his lap and lifted her butt up for him to see, and tried not to let the job she was doing on him with her tickling tongue send him too far to the edge.

"Do you want to get fucked tonight, Alice?"

"Mmmmm," she said noncommittally, running her widened tongue over the tip of his prick, sucking at some pre-cum that emerged from the hole.

"All you need to do is ask. Ask me to fuck you, and I will, for as long as you want. But you have to say 'please fuck me, Sir.' "

Alice stopped licking and shifted off his lap over the bed, looking at him with wide eyes.

"Say 'please fuck me, Sir,' " he repeated.

Alice didn't respond.

Mr. Sinclaire sighed. He bent down and reached for something under the bed; and when he came back up, he was holding wrist and ankle cuffs by lines of chain already attached, and Alice realized he must have prepared for this moment of defiance and hidden them there before she had even entered the room.

She tried to bolt off the bed, but he had anticipated that, too, and caught her around the foot, pulling her back. Before she knew it, she had a leather cuff buckled around her ankle. He quickly grabbed her other leg and cuffed that ankle, too; and then, working against her wild struggles, he turned her around the bed. Working one foot at a time, he connected the chains into hooks in the floor, one next to each corner of the bed, so that her legs were well spread across the mattress.

Her arms were still free, and she tried to twist and fight him off, trapped on her stomach as she was. But he covered her body with his own, pressing her into the mattress, and worked with the ease of experience until both her wrists were cuffed and chained down, too. She was now stretched spread eagled across the bed, completely immobile on her stomach, and utterly at his mercy.

"That's better," he said. Alice looked at him mutinously out of the corner of her eyes. He grinned and moved to the wardrobe.

"I have a new toy I've been waiting to try," he said. She could hear him pulling something out of the wardrobe. "I think now is the perfect time." He returned to show it to her, and Alice's mouth opened in alarm.

It looked almost like a hairbrush on a stick--a vastly altered, fear-inducing hairbrush. The handle was long, a good three feet, obviously to give the wielder a longer reach. At the top, the back of the "brush" was oval and flat, so that the bristles came to an even edge. Alice noticed that the ends of the bristles were slightly rounded and blunted, but even so, they looked painfully sharp.

"Would you like to see how it feels?" Mr. Sinclaire asked her innocently. Again, Alice didn't answer one way or the other. Her host smiled. Then he stepped over... and struck.

WHAP--

Alice shrieked. It felt like a thousand tiny needles had just been pressed into the skin of her soft bottom.

"Hurts?" Mr. Sinclaire tapped the vicious toy against his palm and grinned ominously. "I can imagine. But it doesn't have to. You can make all this stop. Just say 'please fuck me, Sir,' and I'll stop." Alice shook her head into the mattress. Mr. Sinclaire walked over and knelt by her face, until she could feel his hot breath by her ear.

"Ahh, Alice, why do you have to be so proud? It's your pride that keeps you at my mercy." She didn't respond. "Just remember, all you have to do is beg, beg for me to fuck you, and I'll stop." He straightened and walked to her side, raising the brush high into the air. "I think I'll do five at a time," he said. Alice closed her eyes.

WHAP WHAP WHAP WHAP WHAP--

Before the fifth one had even hit, Alice was crying out loudly, her face contorted with fury. Mr. Sinclaire leaned down once more, looking into Alice's flushed face.

"Say it, Alice." Through the tears beginning to stream from her eyes, Alice shook her head no.

WHAP WHAP WHAP WHAP WHAP--

Another five came down on her soft bottom, and Alice struggled against the chains. By the fifth one, she was shrieking. Again, he leaned into her face; but this time, he let his rough cheek brush against her smooth, wet one.

"Say it, Alice," he entreated. Alice turned her head away, shaking from her sobs.

WHAP WHAP WHAP WHAP WHAP--

Their contest of wills went on; and for the first time, Mr. Sinclaire began to worry that Alice might seriously hurt herself. Her bottom was a fiery red now, freckled crimson from the bristles. She wasn't actually bleeding, the skin wasn't broken--yet. But he had no idea how long that would last.

"Say it, Alice," he ordered again after delivering another five, his voice thick with grit. Alice took a long, shuddering breath and turned her face towards his. Her lip quivered, and wisps of her hair stuck to her cheeks; but her eyes smoldered in defiance, burning into his soul. She looked glorious, trapped as she was, still as proud and as beautiful as any goddess on mount Olympus.

WHAP WHAP WHAP WHAP WHAP--

At last, just when Mr. Sinclaire began to fear that she might actually win this particular contest of wills, Alice begged for mercy.

"Please, please, stop, please stop--"

"Say it, Alice," he ordered gently.

"Please fuck me Sir, please fuck me, please--"

Quickly now, Mr. Sinclaire uncuffed her ankles and wrists, while Alice sobbed face down into the bed. After he had finished freeing her limbs, he climbed onto the bed behind her and lifted her by the hips. He separated her legs, took position, and entered her cunt in a single, smooth thrust.

Alice was still crying a little into the mattress, but her cunt was hot and tight and wet, a testament to her own arousal, and it felt wonderful against her host's long, thick prick. Mr. Sinclaire thrusted slowly, moving in and out with measured strokes, savoring the feel of her gripping pussy squeezing all around him.

It took Alice only a few moments to begin to feel the first stirrings of sexual passion return in force. Mr. Sinclaire felt huge inside her constricting pussy, hard and demanding, and the inner walls of her cunt clenched around him instinctively. Her tears subsided, and she turned her face to the side, breathing hard, caught up in rising sexual need.

Alice lifted her weight off her chest and braced herself on her hands. She began to gently rock back and forth on the mattress, meeting his thrusts, trying to match his rhythm and bring herself off.

Grinning widely now, Mr. Sinclaire thoughtfully wet two of his fingers before reaching around and gliding them inside Alice's cunt lips. He rubbed around gently, and when he found his target, he straighted his fingers, rubbing them right across her swollen clitoris. Alice cried out.

"Oh oh oh--"

Mr. Sinclaire thrusted, flicked, squeezed and rubbed...until Alice was rocking her entire body hard on the bed, gliding her squeezing cunt up and down his prodding length, rubbing herself off on his gentle wet fingers and hard swollen cock.

"OH GOD--"

Her whole body convulsed when she came, and she arched up, squeezing Mr. Sinclaire's prick inside her straining, throbbing pussy. Mr. Sinclaire kept going, thrusting harder now, pounding into her; and then Alice came again, right on top of her first orgasm, surprising them both. Her cries of ecstasy and the feel of her clenching grip sent him careening over the edge himself, and he came in a final, powerful lunge.

They both collapsed on the bed, breathing heavily.

Mr. Sinclaire was hesitant to ask if Alice was okay; such a question might be taken the wrong way. But he grazed a finger down her tenderized bottom and gave her a questioning look when she cringed.

"I'll be okay," she said softly. "But tonight... tonight, I'm done."

"You're done? Is that a request to call for the liaison? Shall I have Mr. Brooks bring you back to your room?"

"Well, no, I didn't mean that," she said.

When he furrowed his brows, giving her a crooked grin, she laughed and climbed on top of him, straddling his stomach. Her breasts hung high and proud, her nipples protruding out like delicate pink nubs, and Mr. Sinclaire reached up and held them in his wide hands with splayed fingers. Alice moaned and closed her eyes; then she leaned down and whispered into his ear:

"Fuck me again, Sir. Please, fuck me again."

Deborah

DEBORAH FOLDER WAS AN acquisitions lawyer. Driven by her career, she had already become the youngest associate in her firm's history, and the only woman to have ever done so.

Smart, straightforward, meticulous in her paperwork and aggressive in the way she dealt with contract negotiations, she had gained herself a reputation of being quite the shark. And if, in the quiet pockets of the office hallways, some of her staff called her a bitch, she pretended not to know or care; but many soon suspected that Ms. Folder secretly reveled in her reputation, and the fear she instilled around the office.

But Deborah had other needs, ones her day to day career activities could not fulfill.

She had been married, briefly, years ago; but her husband had disappeared quickly, and rumor had it he had not been able to satiate her appetite, whatever it was her appetite craved. Although she dated, she never stayed exclusive to any one man; they were all used as dinner companions and arm-candy for the many high profile events she was required to attend.

But four times a year she would go on vacation, and when she returned, her staff could sense the difference inside her, the calmness to her mind the trips awarded, if only for a little while. One could not exactly call it *tranquility*; Ms. Folder was never a tranquil woman. But she was slower to rebuke her assistants, and smiled a little more often around the corridors.

No one knew where she went on these vacations. She would mark her calendar as "out of the office" and leave messages on her voicemail informing people she was unavailable; but never did she reveal where she was or what she was up to. Speculation ran rampant throughout the office, of course; curiosity that would never be appeased.

What no one ever learned, nor could ever learn, was that Deborah Folder was spending each one of her vacations at the exact same spot, and enjoying herself quite fully every time: and that location was called the Hotel Bentmoore.

Deborah Folder had been a frequent visitor to the hotel for years. Since her divorce, she knew what she needed from a man was not what civilized society would consider normal, or even healthy. She had gone to a marriage counsellor, who had told her what she needed was medication and therapy. But in her heart, Deborah knew that what she needed could not be handled with drugs or therapy sessions; what she needed was someone learned and experienced in other arts, someone who could understand and satisfy her wild desires. She had, in quick succession, divorced, fired her therapist, and found the Hotel Bentmoore.

Here, four times a year, she was not a shark lawyer, controlling and full of bite; here, she was forced to submit, to give up the control that she wore like a mask in her real life, and bow to a will greater than her own. The relinquishment of the tight mask set her free, and in the safe and hidden confines of the rooms at the Hotel, she found new heights of carnal pleasure.

She had only just checked in to the hotel and was still organizing her toiletries when she heard a knock at the door. It was Mr. Trowlege, her hotel liaison. The Hotel Bentmoore had many such people, who acted as a back-and-forth messenger between guest and host, her "host" being the person Deborah would be meeting later in the day. All communication between guest and host, outside of the activity rooms, of course, had to go strictly through the liaisons.

"Mr. Dean welcomes you, ma'am, and would like to confirm the time, seven o'clock tonight," Mr. Trowlege said in his polite voice. Guests at the Hotel Bentmoore were never called anything other than "sir" or "ma'am" outside the activity rooms; discretion and etiquette were key.

"Please tell him that seven o'clock is fine," Deborah said, her voice smooth. Years of practice kept her from giving any indication of her nervousness, but the anticipation was growing inside her belly, and her pelvis tightened with excitement. She gave no hint of it.

"Very good, ma'am," Mr. Trowlege said. "Will you be dining outside on the terrace with the other guests tonight?"

"No, I think I'll eat in my room. Have it sent here," she replied. "Five o'clock, if you please."

"Five o'clock, of course ma'am," he said. "I will return at the appropriate time to take you to Mr. Dean."

"Thank you," Deborah said softly, revealing for the first time some spark of excitement in her eyes. Mr. Trowlege nodded and left.

Her dinner was brought up at five o'clock sharp, after which Deborah bathed, shaved, and applied a gentle layer of makeup to her face. She had learned, over time, never to over-do the eye makeup. It would only run later.

At two minutes to seven, Mr. Trowlege returned as promised; but this time, he uttered not a word as he swept his arm out to escort her down the hallway. Deborah let her door shut behind her with a soft click; she needed no key. When the time came, Mr. Trowlege would be escorting her back to her room.

As they walked down the quiet corridor, Deborah could feel the electric thrill pulsing through her veins, now familiar every time she walked down these hallways while being escorted to her host. The anticipation heightened her senses now, her nerves barely controlled. For tonight, she would be trying something new, something she had never even attempted with any man; something that would hopefully lead her to fresh and unrestrained heights of pleasure.

As they took the elevator down, Deborah stood behind Mr. Trowlege, who looked straight ahead. Deborah could barely keep still; the adrenaline was flowing freely now. But she kept her composure, and when the elevator doors opened with a tiny bing, she followed the liaison dutifully, a few steps behind.

This hallway was darker, scantily lit by dim ceiling lights. There were no windows, of course; all the activity rooms were located in the subterranean floor, although you wouldn't be able to tell by the thick carpet and custom painted halls. A few doors lined the walls, but Deborah knew she would run into no other guests down here. The only two people who would know she had ever been here tonight would be Mr. Trowlege and her host, Mr. Dean. The hotel kept its secrets well.

Mr. Trowlege pressed a button inside the wall next to a heavy wooden door, and immediately opened it. Then, he moved to the side, careful not to look in, and motioned for Deborah to enter. Without a further look to the liaison, Deborah did so; and as she crossed the threshold, Mr. Trowlege closed the door behind her.

Deborah looked around. She had never been in this room before. Large and well lit, it had many of the equipment pieces she had seen in rooms she had already visited, but some were new to her...although she didn't need to stretch her imagination too far to think what *they* could be used for.

A "T" bar sat in one corner, wrist cuffs and chains attached to both arms and the floor. An inverted "X" bar sat next to it, padded and wide; but it, too, had wrist cuffs already attached to each end. On a small table sat a tray with objects lined neatly inside, but Deborah could not make out what they could be.

"Hello, Deborah." Mr. Dean walked forward out of the shadows, calm and assured. He wore grey trousers, pressed and belted; they hung on his long muscled legs like they had been tailored for him alone. But he wore no shirt. His curling chest hairs, as black as the hair neatly cut on his head, spread across his wide muscles and triangled down his belly, disappearing in a straight line down into his belt.

He crossed his arms in easy confidence; Deborah took notice once more of the wide muscles lining his arms and stomach. Her mouth went dry.

"Hello, Sir," she said, looking down. In this room, with this man, she was Deborah, not Ms. Folder; and he was Sir, not Mr. Dean. He had the authority; she had none. Whatever dignity or mercy she asked for, it would be up to him to grant her.

"We are going to test you for something new tonight. I will take my time to prepare you; there is no need to rush these things. Of course, since this will be a novel experience for you, you may feel the need to say something, cry out. I must insist you remain silent at all times. Any utterance or moan of displeasure will be met with swift punishment. Is that understood?"

"Yes, Sir." Deborah cast her eyes down once more. They both knew this was a secret thrill of hers: to have Mr. Dean do what he would to her, and her unable to object, unable to say a single word of protest. She was on full vocal restriction.

"Very good, Deborah. Now then...undress, please." Mr. Dean did not turn away as he said this, but watched and waited with calm control.

Deborah slowly reached her hands behind her and unzipped her dress, pulling off the sleeves and stepping out of it one foot at a time. Mr. Dean watched her do it, giving no hint of approval or pleasure; but his eyes narrowed, filling with heat.

Deborah gave him a tiny grin. It always excited her to have him watch her undress. He did not look at her as a boss, or a girlfriend, or as an object of beauty to be handled with care; he looked at her as a hot blooded woman, to be controlled with a fair, but strong, hand.

Deborah stripped out of the rest of her clothes and placed them neatly on the shelf next to her. Once she was done, she stood up straight, fully aware of the sight she presented.

Slim shoulders sat over a narrow waist; curving hips flared below, and between them, her pink slit, completely shaved, tingling in moist excitement.

"Come here," Mr. Dean said, uncrossing his arms. The command was a simple one, but Deborah took a ragged breath.

She took the few steps needed to bring her all the way to his chest. Still, it was not close enough for him. He grabbed her by both shoulders and pulled her against his skin, rubbing her nipples against his chest.

He made no move to kiss her, but held her with one hand in the small of her back. With the other, he lowered it between their bodies, and placed it over the thick lips of her pussy.

Using two fingers, he pried her lips open; and then, holding them open, he slipped his middle finger inside.

Deborah inhaled sharply, but no sound came from her throat.

"Very good," Mr. Dean murmured. He jiggled his finger. Deborah's eyes flared. Soon, he was pistoning his finger in and out, and her natural juices were easing his way so that his finger was quickly wet with her slickness. Deborah closed her eyes and leaned into his hand. Mr. Dean continued for a few more moments, then pulled out his finger to cup her mound again.

"You need this, don't you Deborah?"

Deborah did not answer, of course; she was not allowed to. But she looked at him with half hooded eyes and nodded slightly.

"But let us not forget why we are here," Mr. Dean said softly. "Tonight, you are here for something else entirely, and that is precisely what I will be providing you." He pointed across the room. "Up against the bench, please."

With wide eyes, Deborah began to walk up to the bench. The knowledge of what was about to happen between them, what was about to be done *to* her, made her steps heavy and slow.

The bench looked like nothing anyone would sit on. It was just over waist high, long and thickly padded. Even the sides were padded, so that when Deborah pressed her belly up against it, it felt soft against her skin, and she sank a bit into it.

As she folded her body over the bench, she noticed handles on each side, specifically designed for grasping, and she tested them in her small hands. She would need them tonight, she had no doubt about that.

As she lowered herself down onto her belly, her breasts flattened against the cushions beneath her, and her nipples rubbed against the fabric. It felt cool and satiny, and made her nipples tingle in unexpected pleasure. She shifted her weight, rested in, and closed her eyes.

Her butt was sticking up in the air, but her legs were still closed, standing together as they were. She heard movement behind her.

"Open your legs, Deborah," Mr. Dean instructed. Deborah did as he ordered, stepping her feet apart, feeling the soft lips of her delicate pink cunt open slightly.

But it was still not enough for him; he put his hands inside her warm thighs and pressed outward, until her legs were well apart.

Mr. Dean ran his hands over her ass and hips, feeling the soft skin, squeezing it now and then and watching her clench her butt muscles together instinctively. He stopped.

"You will have to control yourself better, Deborah," he said sternly. "You need to relax." Deborah took a deep breath and let it out slowly. This time, when he squeezed her sensitive ass flesh, she kept her butt muscles relaxed, letting him get a good grip on her.

"Better," he said. But instead of releasing her, he pressed his fingers into her pliant mounds and spread her cheeks apart. For a moment, he held her open, revealing her hidden dark places to his gaze.

Despite her embarrassment and discomfort, Deborah willed herself to relax and allow him to look at her as he would. She squeezed the handles tightly, and scrunched up her face; but she kept her legs slack.

"Much better," Mr. Dean said quietly. "We are going to begin now, Deborah. Remember, remain silent at all times."

Deborah took a few shallow breaths. With her head turned to the side as it was, she could not see what was going on behind her; but she could hear, and what she heard was a jar opening. Then Mr. Dean was rubbing his hands together; and then his hands were on her.

At first, his hands, now slick with lubricant, caressed her ass as they had before. But slowly, purposefully, they moved between her cheeks, spreading them apart. This time, while one hand kept her soft and pliant mounds apart, the other began to trace a finger up and down the inside of her crack.

Deborah's squeezed her eyes shut; every time his tickling finger touched her intimate skin, the squeezing ring of her anus, she gasped. Her asshole spasmed and clenched, closing tightly. Mr. Dean let his finger trail where it would, up, down, and around, sometimes using the whole finger pad, sometimes just using the edge of his fingertip.

Now he stopped for a moment, removing the tickling finger, and Deborah held her breath. When his finger returned, it felt cool and slick, and pressed flatly right against her tightly resisting asshole.

Deborah arched her back up; Mr. Dean pushed her back down.

"None of that, now," he said without removing the offending finger away from her squeezing ring of muscle. "Use the handles if you must, but stay *down*."

Deborah did as he instructed, lowering her body back into the bench and grabbing onto the handles. She could feel the nerve endings of her tightening anus sending alarming messages straight to her brain, but she tamped them down, keeping her need to squirm and escape at bay.

Mr. Dean gave her a few moments to get used to the feel of his finger pressing against her puckering asshole. He was in no hurry; as long she listened, followed directions, and obeyed the rules, he would go slow and easy on her. Deborah knew this. She had visited with Mr. Dean many times over the years she had been coming to the Hotel Bentmoore. The hotel encouraged their clients to find a host they could develop a rapport with, someone with whom they could cultivate a sense of trust.

After a few moments, Deborah had gotten somewhat used to the novel sensation of her host's finger touching the sensitive nerves around her ass, and she began to relax. Her legs went limp, and she let out an easy breath.

"Very good," Mr. Dean said. Deborah took that as a sign that her host was now going to move forward in her "preparation," and she was not wrong.

Mr. Dean began to circle her sensitive asshole with his lubricated finger, circling the wrinkled flesh, getting it sticky and slick. Deborah bit her lip. Mr. Dean's finger felt very bold, and very big.

"You have a beautiful ass, Deborah," Mr. Dean remarked as he painted her asshole with the lubricant on his finger. "Nice and tight. You just need to learn to *relax*." As he finished his sentence, he targeted his finger right in the middle of her cringing hole, and pressed in. Taken by surprise, Deborah's head came off the cushions, and she released a tiny yelp.

Immediately, Mr. Dean's hand came up, and smacked her hard against her rump.

SLAP!

Deborah cried out; another stinging slap hit her on her other cheek, matching the first. This time, Deborah buried her face into the cushions and kept quiet. Mr. Dean didn't have to tell her that if she made another sound, another slap would be hitting her soft behind.

"Let's try this again, shall we?" Mr. Dean's voice was low and even.

Again, he used one hand to open her cheeks with splayed fingers. Again, he pressed his index finger to her closed asshole with the other. Deborah pushed her face deeper into the padding, breathing heavily through her mouth.

"Slowly, now," Mr. Dean said comfortingly, like a teacher would to a distressed pupil. "No need to rush. Relax your muscles." Deborah could feel his finger tip just at her opening hole, the mere presence acting as an impertinent intruder. But, closing her eyes and taking controlled, heavy breaths, she did as he bade her, relaxing her ass, so that he could move his finger in ever so slightly before she clenched up once more. As she squeezed reactively, he drew his finger back.

He worked slowly but relentlessly, pressing his finger into her warm channel, drawing back when she squeezed, giving her a second to collect herself and relax, then pressing in again. Each time, he was able to poke his finger in a little bit more, slipping in wetly, until he had passed the thick ring of muscle and could wiggle his first knuckle deep inside her warm, tight channel. Deborah squeezed the bench handles tightly; a groan almost escaped her lips, but she held it back.

Once he was passed her gate of resistance, Mr. Dean eased in, pushing his finger all the way up her ass in a single, bold push.

"There we are," he said in a gentle voice. Mr. Dean pressed the knuckles of his hand into her flesh, so she would know she now had his entire finger up her ass. He twisted his finger inside her; Deborah clenched instinctively. But this time, her host did not draw back, but kept twisting as Deborah's ass clenched and throbbed.

Her mouth opened wide, and tears sprang to her eyes; but slowly, as Mr. Dean's finger screwed in, Deborah calmed down, letting the feel of his skewering finger take over her nerves. She could think of nothing, feel nothing, save that impertinent finger deep inside her, wreaking havoc with her senses.

The tickling discomfort receded, as her body accustomed itself to the finger deep inside her rectum. Pleasure began to surface in her mind, and Deborah relaxed completely, enjoying the feel of Mr. Dean's finger straightening and coiling inside her.

Once he had lubricated her as far up as his finger would allow, Mr. Dean slowly pulled his finger out, Deborah hissing between her teeth as it went.

"You are doing very well, Deborah," Mr. Dean said encouragingly. "Let's move on, shall we?" He removed his hands from her for a moment, and Deborah could hear him retrieve something from the tray. When he stepped up behind her once more, Deborah could hear a juicy sliding motion; Mr. Dean was rubbing something with more lubricant. What it could be, she had no idea.

"I'm afraid you are going to feel very slick after this, my dear," he said. "But since this is your first time, it is important to ease the way. Let out your breath, now." Deborah had been holding it while listening to him glide his hands over--whatever it was he was holding in his hands. She released it now, slowly, all her muscles tensing up.

And once again, Mr. Dean spread her cheeks apart. Something cold, almost sharp, poked against her asshole. Deborah wanted to say something, to object; but she knew what would happen if she did.

The rules set between her and Mr. Dean had been established long before; any defiance she raised now would be met with swift punishment. And ultimately, deep down, that's what Deborah wanted--that was why she was here. To be nurtured but controlled, pampered when she was good but forced to submit when the time came; to have the heights of forbidden pleasure forced upon her, no matter what she might say, or how hard her sense of propriety might react against it.

Gently, Deborah could feel Mr. Dean pressing the object into her tight ass.

"This is an anal dildo," he said, as if making polite conversation. "It gets wider at the end...it's made of crystal. I like crystal. It warms up to body temperature quite quickly." As he spoke, he continued to press the hard dildo into Debra's lubricated, clenching ass.

At first, it felt thinner than his finger had; but quickly, it began to widen, forcing her hole to open more as it slipped in. Soon it felt thick and completely unforgiving, dilating her straining anus until she thought she couldn't stretch any further. Her sensitive flesh began to throb; she could feel the blood rushing to her overfilled ass. Mr. Dean stopped.

"This is the hard part, Deborah," he said. "You're almost there. Don't fight it." With a single finger, he tapped the base of the crystal anal dildo, every so lightly; but her straining hole ached painfully in response.

Each time he tapped, he hammered the anal dildo further up her warm channel. Bit by bit, he nailed it into her, watching it disappear up her widening rectum. But it was too much; Deborah couldn't take the painful stretching anymore. She arched her back and cried out.

Mr. Dean's hand came down on the sloping hill of her ass with a loud crack. But the anal rod was still pressing hard into Deborah's ass, and when she tightened up from the slap, her butt muscles instinctively squeezed around the thick dildo, making it feel twice as big as before.

He tapped the dildo again; she cried out again; he slapped her other butt cheek even harder, then slapped the first one again for good measure. Mr. Dean's hands were very wide and very hard, calloused and rough from years of proper use, and they left angry red blushes across Deborah's smooth skin. He never used whips or paddles, at least not on Deborah. From the beginning, Mr. Dean had made it clear that there would be no barriers between his will and her skin.

Tears fell from Deborah's eyes; she breathed raggedly into the padding.

Mr. Dean gave Deborah a second to gather herself, then continued his relentless tapping on the base of the rod. Deborah could do nothing but let the pain wash over her, sending her into a place of pure submission, feeling all sense of control slip away completely. Colors danced in front of her eyes; her body could not move, but her mind was free, and she floated away, feeling nothing but the intermittent electric shocks pulsating from her ass every time her host tapped on the stubborn rod.

At last, she felt the thing slip in...and stop. At the very end, the rod narrowed greatly before widening again at the base, leaving the thickest and widest part swallowed up inside Deborah's stretched rectum. She could clench and bear down all she wanted; that unforgiving dildo was not going anywhere.

"It's in," Mr. Dean said. "Go ahead and get a good feel for it, Deborah. Just keep your body bent over the bench." He moved away from her a step, giving her space.

Deborah shifted her feet from side to side, feeling the unyielding dildo touch different nerve endings deep inside her every time she moved. She couldn't get away from it, she couldn't escape the strange, tight, burning sensations coming from her asshole...and after a few minutes, she didn't want to.

The blood throbbing in her ass was rushing to her head, making her feel dizzy and weak. Pain gave way to pleasure as the ache subsided.

Deborah felt very stuffed, and the dildo was tickling her innards in a way that filled her with wanton need. She began to rock her hips back and forth, holding onto the handles for support.

"I think you like it now, don't you?" Mr. Dean asked from behind her. Deborah could only nod her head in acquiescence. He pulled her by the hips and pressed his palm into the base of the rod; Deborah rocked back against it, itching to reach her hand up between her legs and touch herself. But she dared not; Mr. Dean had not given her leave to do so. So she continued to rock, feeling the maddening itch, the desperate need.

"Are you ready to come now, Deborah?"

Deborah picked up her head from the bench and nodded vigorously. Her host paused.

"You must ask permission to come with the dildo up your ass," he ordered. "Ask nicely, Deborah."

"Please, Sir, please I want to come with the dildo in my ass," Deborah said.

"Not in your ass--up your ass," Mr. Dean corrected her.

"Up my ass, I want to come with the dildo up my ass, please Sir," Deborah pleaded, the need growing to a fever pitch inside her. The maddening tickle coming from deep inside her asshole was sending her to the edge.

"Very well," her host replied, handing her another toy, this time a circular vibrating one. He obligingly turned it on before handing it to her. "You may use this. Go on. Make yourself come!"

Deborah reached for the toy and, still bent over the bench, held it to her slightly opened cunt lips, right against her swollen clitoris. As soon as she felt the humming vibrator against the focal point of her pleasure, she moaned loudly; and this time, Mr. Dean did not smack her bottom in response. Only when he allowed her to come was she also allowed to make all the noise she wanted.

"Oh god oh god oh god--" She bucked her hips back and forth against the bench as the two toys, one ensconced up her ass, the other vibrating happily between her pussy lips, sent her over the edge of the abyss. All her sinews tightened in response; her legs stretched up, pushing her further up the bench; a plaintive moan bolted from her mouth.

And Mr. Dean watched, enthralled, as her asshole spasmed rhythmically around the dildo, trying to pull it even deeper into her ass. But the flaring base held it in place, tightly pressed into her soft cheeks.

In the last moment, Mr. Dean pressed his hand against the base, shoving the rod further in, and getting a high pitched shriek in response. Deborah came wildly, bucking her hips, thrusting back and forth against the bench.

After a few long moments, Deborah's breathing evened out, and her body relaxed. Even so, her asshole squeezed against the offending dildo, kissing the crystal in loving homage. But the hand holding the vibrating toy against her wet cunt fell to the floor.

And all the while, Mr.Dean remained behind her, watching her reactions, taking in her every move. Deborah knew that every time she visited with Mr. Dean, he took careful notice of her responses, making mental notes to himself for the next time.

Once her breathing had quieted down, Mr. Dean took the humming toy from her hand, turned it off, and placed it back on the tray.

"Relax now, Deborah--this will hurt more if you tighten up. Hold on to the handles again."

Deborah closed her eyes and gripped the handles of the bench tightly, as Mr. Dean slowly eased the warm anal dildo out of her ass. The hardest part was also the start, getting the widest radius of the dildo past her clenching muscle; but once it was out, the rest came smoothly. Deborah breathed a sigh of relief.

"You did very well tonight, Deborah," Mr. Dean said in approval. "You may get up now and get dressed." Deborah stretched herself up, feeling very loose and slippery inside. She looked up at her host, who had a large bulge inside his pants, but otherwise, seemed unaffected by everything he had just been doing to his guest. Deborah knew this was just another sign of Mr. Dean's incredible control.

Deborah walked over to where her dress sat folded, waiting. Her ass ached a little, but surprisingly, not as much as she had thought it would. Of course, this was only her first day, her "preparation." Next would come tomorrow....

"I will see you again tomorrow, seven o'clock," Mr. Dean said, as if he could read her thoughts. "The liaison will give you any further instructions, should I feel the need to give them."

Deborah nodded. "Thank you, Sir," she said softly.

Once she was dressed, Mr. Dean walked over to the door and pressed a button in the wall. All the activity rooms were sound proof, of course; but by pressing the button, he let Mr. Trowlege know from somewhere else deep in the bowels of the hotel that Ms. Folder was now ready to be escorted back to her room.

Deborah only had to wait a few moments before the door opened, and Mr. Trowlege was there waiting at the side, ready for her to walk through.

"Thank you, Sir," Deborah said again, looking her host shyly. Mr. Dean only nodded at her with half hooded eyes as the door closed.

*****

The next day, Deborah was brought to Mr. Dean again. But this time, it was to a different room; and this room didn't have quite so many strange apparatus inside, except for the very unusual table sitting in the middle.

The table was thickly padded. But toward the end, the legs began to diverge, so that it formed an upside down V. At the moment, the legs were opened only slightly, but it looked as if the entire thing were adjustable, so that the legs, head, or whole table, could be raised and lowered. And there were grip handles set in each side, Deborah noticed--but no cuffs, and no chains.

Of course, chains could be added if necessary, Deborah thought fleetingly. But Mr. Dean had no use for chains, at least not with her. She obeyed his commands as his rules dictated, because if she did not, she would suffer the consequences, and suffer them she had over the years.

More than once Mr. Dean had put her over his knee and given her the spanking of her life, until she had been reduced to sniveling, cowering submission. She used to fight it, struggle against him until she had to submit. But she always *did* submit, eventually.

She was never allowed to leave this room until Mr. Dean decided they were done, activity completed... and that always meant Deborah had to submit completely. It was up to Mr. Dean to decide when she had done enough, completed the task at hand to his liking; her wishes meant nothing.

Of course, she could always refuse the enter the room at all. Coming here was completely voluntary. But it was what she needed: to relinquish all control to this man, who knew how to send her to a place in her mind where thoughts could not penetrate, where only feelings existed and clouds of colors floated in and out. When she crossed the threshold of this room, she also crossed a threshold in her mind, and there was no going back-- from either.

Mr. Dean was waiting for her as usual, coming out of the shadows as the door closed.

"Did you have a nice day, Deborah? Didn't spend too much time being anxious, I hope?" Sometimes, he began like this, making small talk with her as if they were here for no other reason than polite conversation, while other times, he got right down to business.

"A little, Sir," she admitted.

He kept his expression neutral. "Well. It's to be expected. The first time is always about experience. But let us not keep you waiting in dread any longer. Undress and go to the table, please."

He watched her undress, as he always did: he had made it clear right from the beginning of their arrangement that there would be no part of her body she had the right to keep from his eyes. If he wanted her to bend in any way to get a better view of her peaks and valleys, well then, that was what she would have to do. Over the years, she had become something of a contortionist.

But tonight there was bigger business to take care of than making Deborah exhibit for him. She quickly shimmied out of her clothes and walked over to the strange table, but stopped at the side. She didn't know quite how she was supposed to get on.

"Climb up on your hands and knees," Mr. Dean breathed in her ear. Deborah jumped a little; her nerves were on edge. "Relax," her host whispered, pulled a wisp of hair away from her neck.

He reached around and cupped her breast. Her chest heaved with her deep breathing; he held her breast in his wide square hand and rubbed her nipple with the pad of his thumb. Deborah shut her eyes and swayed back. Already, she could feel herself slipping into total submission.

"On the table, Deborah," Mr. Dean said, and took a step to push her slightly toward the table.

Deborah crawled onto it, maneuvering herself on her hands and knees so that her legs lay centered on the padded V. Her light, pear shaped breasts wobbled a little as she got into position, dipping down heavily once she was on, her nipples growing hard as they brushed against the padding.

Mr. Dean, still by her side, maneuvered her stance even more, so that her shoulders drooped slightly into the table, making her ass present higher. Then, he moved behind her and spread the legs of the table, separating them far enough so that he fit snugly between them, right up against her presenting ass.

"Don't move, Deborah," he warned. She heard him rustling around behind her, heard a mechanism being turned; and then the whole table was being lowered down, while Mr. Dean kept her steady with his warm, calloused hands on her hips, until he had her at just the height he wanted. Deborah swallowed and squeezed her eyes shut. She understood, now, exactly what level her hips were at...and her ass....

"I think, tonight, I will allow you to raise your voice a little--just enough to make some noise, you understand. Such a new experience, we must make some allowances to honor it, and experience it appropriately."

"Thank you, Sir," Deborah breathed, still looking at the wall straight ahead. He had let go of her hips, and she wondered what he was doing back there.

The question was answered soon enough when he lay a warm, steady hand on her backside, and slipped the other right inside the crack of her ass.

The shock of it sent her jerking forward. The edge of his hand snuggled neatly between her cheeks, pushing against her anus. And it was already slick with lubricant: he had rubbed his whole hand with it thoroughly before laying it in her.

Mr. Dean put an arm around her hips and pulled her back, making her elbows give.

"Shoulders down!" He said. "There are handles on the sides to grab onto if you need them. I am giving you warning, Deborah, I will allow some vocalization out of you tonight...but *do not move*."

And right there was the price for his generosity, the catch she had been waiting for. She could make some noise, cry out if she needed to--but she could not jerk away. She could not move at all. There would be no escape.

"Yes, Sir," Deborah said, her throat dry. She was nervous, so nervous she was almost trembling with it, and yet, she was nervous with anticipation, too. There was no going back now--she would have to get through whatever her host put her through for the rest of this night. And tonight...tonight, he would be leading her down a new path, and hopefully, to new heights.

Mr. Dean lazily began rubbing his hand up and down the valley between Deborah's soft, perfectly rounded hills, occasionally touching the soft folds of her delicate pink pussy, but for the most part, ignoring it completely. His thick thumb pressed against her spasming asshole, pressing in quickly. Before Deborah could react, it had slipped in up to the knuckle.

"Ah," Deborah inhaled sharply. She sank her shoulders down all the way into the padding and shifted her head to the side, but was careful not to move her hips away from Mr. Dean's prying thumb. Instead, she reached down the sides of the table to grab onto the handles.

Behind her, Mr. Dean's thumb pressed forward with its rude assault, pushing into her vulnerable sphincter and wiggling now and then for good measure. Deborah tried to relax and release her muscles; and whenever she did, Mr. Dean's slow assault on her ass would press on.

He didn't pull back when she clenched, the way he did last night; instead, he stopped and waited. He moved his finger around inside, bending it at the knuckle and twisting it, so that he could feel her delicate, dilating tissue all around his finger.

She hurt, and her ass throbbed...but slowly, his thumb disappeared up her ass, until it was up all the way in, to his palm.

"Ahh, Deborah, I can feel your heartbeat inside. You have such a marvelous ass," Mr. Dean said. Deborah didn't reply; it was all she could do to keep herself still. With his finger thick and hard inside her, she felt impaled on his thumb. She wanted to crawl forward, she wanted to rock on her hands and knees...she wanted to *move*. She could not.

Mr. Dean gave his thumb a last brazen twist, making Deborah suck in her breath again, and then he slowly began to ease out the daring digit. It came out smoothly, but Deborah could still feel every bump and knuckle.

Now Deborah could hear Mr. Dean pulling on his belt buckle; the belt being yanked from his trousers; the distinctive sounds of her host removing his clothes...and slick rubbing.

"Breathe, Deborah," Mr. Dean instructed. Deborah tried, she really did. But the adrenaline was rushing through her bloodstream now, and she was quivering with nervousness.

Mr. Dean put both his hands on her hips, biting into the flesh a bit. It was not just to keep her steady: it was to let her know in no uncertain terms that what she was about to feel against her constricting asshole was definitely not one of his fingers, but a much bigger, and much more demanding presence.

Mr. Dean rubbed his cock up and down her smooth valley for a moment, letting her get a feel of his hard prick against her skin. Then, he zeroed in on her tiny spasming asshole, and pushed.

It didn't begin thin and small, the way the anal rod had the day before; the head of his cock felt huge, monstrous against her tiny gate. Even so, with the ease of the lubricant and Mr. Dean's steady pressure, the bulbous head slowly began to be swallowed up by Deborah's ass.

Her anus throbbed and burned by the sudden impalement. But it wasn't the discomfort that finally broke Deborah's composure: it was the knowledge of what she was *allowing*, of what was about to be done *to* her. *She was about to be taken up the ass.*

Her eyes flared, and she lunged forward. Behind her, Mr. Dean was literally jerked out of her ass, which hurt her more than the insertion had.

Realizing what she had just done, Deborah looked behind her at Mr. Dean, who was of course naked, and sporting a proud erection.

"I'm sorry Sir, I'm sorry, I just couldn't, please--" Without breaking their eye contact, Mr. Dean reached under the V legs of the table and lowered them both, so that Deborah's waist was suddenly resting on the edge of the bench, and her legs were dangling down to the floor. Mr. Dean moved beside her.

"Please--"

SLAP!

"Oh--"

SLAP!

Mr. Dean raised his hand and let fly again, smacking her twice on the right cheek. Those slaps hurt like hell, but nothing like the next one he delivered to her left cheek. Deborah yelled and shrieked. Her host ignored her cries.

SLAP! SLAP! SLAP! SLAP!

He kept walloping her, hitting her again and again, following his own rhythm, giving Deborah the barest moment to feel the impact of the last slap before he let the next hit. He alternated between butt cheeks, but kept his hands centered on the highest swells of her ass, until Deborah was crying and pleading for mercy.

"Please, Sir, please, please...." Her voice became plaintive and high pitched. Mr. Dean didn't stop, but placed his other hand on the small of her back to keep her still, while Deborah struggled and writhed.

At last, when Deborah's legs went slack and her face softened in defeat, Mr. Dean stopped. Deborah had entered a state of complete submission All her psychological barriers had been beaten away, until she had no shred of resistance left.

She took a deep breath. Mr. Dean raised the legs of the table and helped Deborah put her legs back up; her knees were quivering and weak. He widened the V of her legs again, giving himself more room between them, and held her by the thighs as she slowly lowered her shoulders down, assuming the position.

This time, when he put the head of his cock at the entrance to her back gate, Deborah kept her muscles slack, taking deep breaths to calm herself completely as her host's dick poked her from behind. It eased in, thick and hard, and Deborah bit her lip. With her eyes closed, she felt for the handles down the sides of the table and grabbed on, pulling her chest, and her breasts, deeper into the padding.

Mr. Dean drove in slowly, stopping completely when she clenched too hard, letting her muscles naturally suck him in. He kept up his steady assault on her ass until the very end, when he lunged the wide base of his cock all the way in her, stretching her throbbing asshole painfully.

"Ahh," Deborah cried out; but it was done. He was in. Mr. Dean circled his hips against her stinging blushing butt, letting her know she had him all, his complete length inside her.

Then, slowly, he eased out, until only the helmeted tip of his prick was still inside. He took a quick breath and lunged; Deborah lifted her head and moaned.

"On your hands, Deborah," Mr. Dean ordered now. Deborah let go of the handles and raised herself to her hands, while Mr. Dean kept hold of her hips. He was thrusting in and out of her with steady, even strokes.

The burning discomfort Deborah had felt in the beginning was quickly disappearing as Mr. Dean's cock rubbed against the sensitive rim of her ass; and with each stroke, a jolt of pleasure passed through her, making her legs tremble and her anus constrict around his hard member even more.

Behind her, Mr. Dean was beginning to grunt quietly, but kept his tempo and the strength of his thrusts in complete control.

He reached underneath her to grab her dangling breasts.

"Touch yourself, Deborah," he said. "Reach your hand under you and rub your clit."

Deborah immediately did what he bade her. Long ago, when she had first started to visit the Bentmoore Hotel and Mr. Dean, Deborah had been too ashamed and dignified to touch herself in front of any man; but years under Mr. Dean's heavy hand had quickly rid her of that inhibition.

Deborah locked an elbow in to steady herself, and began to rub her clit between her pussy lips.

Soon, she was thrusting back against Mr. Dean's stroking cock, forcing him deeper into her ass, as she rubbed her fingers against her clit with increasing frenzy. Mr. Dean held onto her ass now, thrusting strongly, feeling the pulse of her rushing blood throbbing tightly around his swollen cock. He was on the edge, he knew, but would hold himself back until Deborah came.

She did quickly, rubbing her clit madly, her hand almost completely hidden inside her slick and swollen pussy lips. She moaned and lifted her head, arched and bended her back, rocking hard on hand and knees so that Mr. Dean's cock was flowing in and out of her asshole easily, making wet sucking noises with each lunge. Her body shuddered and convulsed as the first orgasmic wave exploded inside her.

"Ah ah AH--" She lunged herself back, hard; and in that moment, Mr. Dean came, erupting his shooting cock right into Deborah's tight, warm rectum. In the split second he did, his prick seemed to harden even more, ramming into Deborah's ass like a steel rod, and Deborah was hit by another wave of ecstasy; she shrieked and pulled up. Mr. Dean pulled her back by the hips, burying himself inside her spasming asshole, until he was thoroughly depleted himself.

When the waves of pleasure had finished hitting her and only small aftershocks still jolted her wracked body, Deborah sank her chest into the padding, her breathing heavy and ragged. Mr. Dean pulled his shrinking and dripping cock out of her spasming asshole, but Deborah didn't even react. She was still recovering from her own intense release. She lowered her stomach down until she was laying flat, trying to catch her breath.

Mr. Dean staggered back away from her splayed legs, holding onto the table for support. He recovered faster than Deborah did, though, and quickly went to a table in the corner to grab a towel and clean himself off a bit. Then he came back and bent next to Deborah's head.

"Was I...good?" Deborah asked, raising her head to look at him. She desperately wanted to hear his words of approval.

"Yes, you were good," Mr. Dean answered, a hint of a smile playing across his lips. "Tell me, was it as bad as you were so afraid it would be?"

"No, not at all," she said. "At least, not after the... beginning."

"We build up the fear in our minds, until it's the fear holding us back, not the act," Mr. Dean said gently. "I want you to remember that, think about it before you return tomorrow. Come, get up." He gave her a hand to steady herself as she stood. Then he kissed her on the lips, lightly, and ran his hand across her butt. It felt like sandpaper against her skin, red and stinging as it was from the spanking, but she didn't wiggle away. Instead, she turned away shyly, pulling her dress on with fluent fingers.

Behind her, Mr. Dean did not pull his pants on, but retrieved a robe from the wardrobe in the corner and belted it around his lean, muscled body. As soon as Deborah was done getting dressed, he pushed the button inside the wall by the door, and they waited silently until Mr. Trowlege swung it wide for her to leave.

But before she walked through, her host had one last parting message for her.

"Don't make me punish you again tomorrow, Deborah," Mr. Dean said. "It would only embarrass you in front of our guest."

"Yes, Sir," Deborah said softy. "Thank you, Sir." She always thanked him on the way out. It was the polite thing to do.

*****

The next day, Deborah woke up late, and spent the entire afternoon by the pool, soaking up the sun rays and otherwise just relaxing. There were many things to do inside and around the hotel, such as tennis and horseback riding, but Deborah was not into those kinds of sports.

She liked to relax and let her mind wander on these little vacations of hers. She had enough competitive games going on in her real life.

Only once that day was her relaxation momentarily interrupted, by a pool boy briskly walking up to where she was lying in her lounge chair, almost asleep. She was on her stomach, letting the heat of the sun warm her back and legs in her bikini top and skirted bottom (her pert little ass cheeks were still somewhat red from the night before), and was already dozing when she heard a pair of feet run up and stop by her head. She lowered her sunglasses a fraction and looked up.

"A message, ma'am," the young man said; he looked to be fresh into his twenties. He was wearing only a pair of swim shorts, and Deborah could see every hard line of his body. The hotel was very discriminate whom they hired...and for what position.

He held a small tray in his hand, upon which sat a sealed envelope. Deborah took it and neatly ripped it open. After reading the message inside, she carefully put the short letter back inside the envelope, and replaced it onto the tray.

"Any message back, ma'am?"

"Just say it's fine," she answered, pushing her glasses back up on her face. The pool boy's feet turned and disappeared.

The rest of the day Deborah tried to relax, but as nervous as she was, it was almost a relief when the time finally came for Mr. Trowlege to collect her from her room.

This time, he took her all the way down the darkened hallway, almost to the very last room. Deborah could not remember if she had ever been to this activity room before. Not that it mattered; the rooms were constantly being rearranged, with equipment added or exchanged, depending on the needs of the host.

As usual, Mr. Trowlege pressed a button before swinging the door wide, and Deborah experienced that second of hesitation before she walked across the threshold, fully aware that she was about to cross a point of no return. Sometimes, she walked through with a smile on her lips, happily anticipating her fate in that room. But other times, like today, Deborah had to close her eyes and will herself the strength just to take that final step inside.

Mr. Trowlege shut the door, and Deborah opened her eyes.

She was in what looked like a large and elegantly modified living room, with soft carpet and plush furniture. Stuffed lounge chairs sat here and there, and a long divan sprawled in the corner. But the focal point of the room was the grand square platform in the middle, like a center stage, lined on every side with pillows. A thick mattress fit snugly onto the low wooden stage, enveloped in a crimson silk sheet. The thing could almost be called a bed, except that it was larger than any bed Deborah had ever seen, low to the ground, and completely square. There were also no blankets; but of course, no one would be sleeping here tonight.

Leaning against one of the lounge chairs was Mr. Dean, dressed as he always was in grey trousers. But a drink rested comfortably in his hand, and he was smiling. On the opposite chair sat another man, the other guest to their little repartee: Mr. Sinclaire.

The note the pool boy had brought Deborah that afternoon had been from Mr. Trowlege, letting her know that Mr. Dean had chosen Mr. Sinclaire as their other guest for the evening. Deborah knew Mr. Sinclaire; she had participated in some activities with him, before she had started visiting Mr. Dean exclusively. He was not quite what Deborah needed on a regular basis, he did not fulfill her wilder needs; but he was professional and creative.

He was also very, very big. Deborah remembered the impressive size and length of his cock, how surprised she had been at first sight, and she bit her lip in nervousness.

Mr. Dean would not have chosen Mr. Sinclaire unless he thought Deborah could handle him; she had to trust her host. Mr. Dean never gave her more than what she could take, often surprising Deborah herself with what she could do...given the proper incentive.

Mr. Dean and Mr. Sinclaire both stood up straight when they noticed her walking in, taking in her breathtaking form. She had decided to dress a bit more provocatively tonight, in honor of the occasion.

Her dress was raspberry pink, more like a robe than a dress, uniquely tailored so that it hung onto her body by thin spaghetti straps, tied together above each shoulder. The sleeves hung low down her arms, showing off the rising swells of her breasts. The dress hung loosely, but tightened around her waist, showing off her curves. By the looks the two men were giving her, she knew they both heartily approved her attire.

Mr. Dean put his drink down on a small side table and walked over.

"You look lovely, my dear," he said, kissing her lightly on the mouth. He took her hand. "I believe you already know Mr. Sinclaire?"

"Yes, Sir."

Mr. Sinclaire looked Deborah over with smoldering eyes and a satisfied grin, but said nothing. Where Mr. Dean was dark, Mr. Sinclaire was light, with blond schoolboy looks and a winning smile. He was a fraction taller than Mr. Dean, and slightly leaner, more wiry. He wore the same tailored trousers Mr. Dean did, but they were blue, not grey, and creased down the legs. Deborah took this all in with adrenaline-heightened senses.

"Mr. Sinclaire is going to be our guest for tonight, Deborah," Mr. Dean said. "It is very important that he be well satisfied by the end of our evening. Don't you agree?"

"Yes, Sir," Deborah said timidly. It didn't exactly matter anymore if she agreed or not, she knew. But Mr. Dean was making the tone of the evening very clear: she would not be leaving until Mr. Dean had decided she had done a good enough job pleasing their other guest. They would be following a loose plan, of course, decided in advance and guided by Mr. Dean; but it was no longer just her pleasure alone that her host was taking into consideration. Deborah licked her lips.

"That dress looks beautiful on you, Deborah, but I don't think we need it anymore. Take it off, please."

Deborah stepped away from the two men and pulled on the spaghetti straps, letting the dress fall to the floor. She stepped out of the puddle of material by her feet and picked it up, tossing it onto a chair beside her.

She wore nothing underneath. Both men took a moment to admire her clean lines and womanly contours.

"Mr. Sinclaire obviously approves of how you handle yourself, Deborah," Mr. Dean said evenly. "But why don't you take him over to the bed and show him what you can do with your mouth? I'm sure he would appreciate that even more."

"Yes, Sir," Deborah complied, walking over to the large platform and crawling onto it as Mr. Sinclaire followed behind. They made their way over to the very center of the padded stage, and knelt up on their knees. Mr. Sinclaire's pants now had a huge bulge straining the hem of the zipper; Deborah remembered again how large this particular man was.

"Go ahead, lower his pants, Deborah," Mr. Dean said encouragingly. "He won't bite."

With light fingers, Deborah unbuckled Mr. Sinclaire's belt and opened his trousers. Lowering them down, Mr. Sinclaire's enormous cock sprang free, and Deborah sucked in her breath.

She lowered her head down, slowly, eyeing her target like a viper ready to strike; and when she got close enough, she kissed the tip of his cock with her moist, soft lips, then opened them just enough to let him slide inside her warm, welcoming mouth.

Mr. Sinclaire groaned softly and dug his hands into her hair. Her mouth was hot and snug, and felt wonderful sliding up and down his long shaft. But Deborah was using her tongue, too, circling his cock inside her mouth, licking it with a deft touch, making sucking motions as she took in as much as she could of his long member down her throat. Mr. Sinclaire tilted his head back and closed his eyes; but after a few blissful moments, he pulled his wet cock away from her face.

"I think Mr. Sinclaire is perhaps enjoying your oral talents a little too much," Mr. Dean said next to them. "The point is to get him wet and ready, Deborah, not finish him off and cheat him of tonight's activities. That would be rude of us, would it not?"

"Yes Sir," Deborah agreed, smiling. It felt good, bringing a man so close to losing all control over his desire for her. She felt powerful and sexy, fully aware of her womanly charms. Mr. Dean's smile disappeared.

"Take his pants off, let him touch you," Mr. Dean ordered them both.

Deborah lowered Mr. Sinclaire's pants until they reached his knees, and then Mr. Sinclaire finished the job, pulling them off completely and throwing them onto a chair nearby.

He overlapped her body with his own, covering hers completely, and took one of her nipples in his mouth, gently sucking on the sensitive pink flesh, flicking it with his tongue. When it felt hard and swollen in his mouth and Deborah was squirming with delight, he switched over, doing the same job on the other nipple that seemed to stand at the ready, waiting its turn.

With all this worshipping nipple stimulation, Deborah was writhing on the bed, thrusting her hips up to try to get Mr. Sinclaire's cock inside her. Finally, he moved between her parted thighs and positioned himself at the entrance to her wet, hot core, and entered her slowly, first just the bulbous head, then shoving in his long, veined prick. Deborah lay back and sighed in delight.

Mr. Sinclaire propped himself up on his elbows and moved his hips in a steady, even, in-and-out motion. The point was not to come. Deborah was not to reach that ultimate carnal delight, not just yet. But she was enjoying herself, oh yes; each thrust brought him deeper inside her, making her stretch and loosen inside, until it felt like he had reached the very core of her womb.

After a few delicious moments, Mr. Dean stopped them both.

"Turn over, switch places," he said, his voice a low growl. "Deborah must be on top now."

Deborah and Mr. Sinclaire passed each other a look, and then Mr. Sinclaire flopped down so that Deborah could climb on top. But he did not stay in the middle of the bed; they had to reposition if they were to move forward in this activity Deborah had specifically requested from her long-time host.

Mr. Sinclaire moved to the very end of the mattress, letting his knees bend over the edge as he lay on his back, arms out. And Deborah straddled his stomach, so that her own feet went slightly over the edge. Her butt was resting on the length of his cock.

Mr. Sinclaire glanced at Mr. Dean.

"Go ahead," Mr. Dean nodded, and Mr. Sinclaire raised Deborah up with strong hands and guided her onto his prick.

It felt huge and heavenly, and Deborah wanted very badly to rock. But she sighed and closed her eyes, feeling deliciously stuffed.

Mr. Dean moved behind her, and Deborah's nerves jolted in alarm; this was the moment of truth, the moment she would either fight and try to escape, or submit to with calm complacency. But she felt so stretched inside already--how was she supposed to take even more?

"Lean forward, Deborah," Mr. Dean said.

Deborah could hear the distinctive sounds of him removing his pants. Then he was opening a jar and making slick rubbing noises, sounds Deborah could now recognize for what they were and make her tremble with worry.

Below her, Mr. Sinclaire grabbed Deborah by the tits and pulled her down until she lay on top of him, her nipples rubbing against his chest hair. He encircled her with his large arms, holding her still, and trapping her down.

Deborah's knees had been splayed across his, and now Mr. Sinclaire widened his legs even further, opening the crack between Deborah's quivering legs wide, letting the air hit her usually hidden flesh. She could actually feel her asshole cringing in alarm. Mr. Sinclaire was still hard and high up inside Deborah's pussy. She was tightening it now in quivering fear.

Mr. Dean placed his hands on Deborah's hips to steady her.

"Relax, Deborah, just like before," he said softly. "Let it happen." Deborah willed herself to relax; she closed her eyes and took deep breaths, trying to calm her nerves. Mr. Dean rubbed his blood engorged cock up and down her sensitive breach, lubricating her with his slick helmeted head, letting her get a feel of him around her winking, shrinking asshole. Finally, he set the head to his target, and pressed in.

Deborah's face scrunched up and her breath came out in a hiss. Mr. Sinclaire, noticing Deborah's reaction, tightened his grip around her to keep her from moving; but he also reached between their bodies and, with one hand, rubbed her nipples, trying to distract her.

But there was no way to distract her from the burning, swollen prick-rod that was now trying to slowly ram her ass. She clenched up instinctively, trying to expel the bold intruder, and still he came on, forcing his way in, until his wide cock was oozing in past her sphincter gate, making her delicate tissues throb and burn in protest.

Deborah let out a high-pitched moan. Mr. Dean stopped.

"Reach behind you and grab your ass cheeks; open them," Mr. Dean ordered. Deborah's eyes widened in surprise. This was not expected.

"Do it, Deborah. Open your ass for me," Mr. Dean ordered more sharply this time. Mr. Sinclaire looked up at her expectantly.

Deborah was trapped. She knew what would happen if she did not do what Mr. Dean had ordered. But it was one thing to have her host use her like this, force her to accommodate him up her throbbing rectum...it was another to have to take part in her own degradation, actively help him as he took her up the ass....

Deborah balanced herself on Mr. Sinclaire's chest and, reaching around, grabbed her ass-flesh. She dug her fingers into her dark crevasse, pulling her ass cheeks apart, opening herself wider to the man wedged between them. As she pulled, she could feel her sphincter trying to squeeze in protest. But it only served to tighten the grip around Mr. Dean's pulsing cock.

Under the control of her own shaking grip, her muscles slowly released, loosening for Mr. Dean's straining prick. As Deborah breathed heavily, trying to relax her manually dilated asshole, Mr. Dean lunged in, pounding her ass against his pelvis. He plugged her sphincter completely, and her asshole stretched and stung.

Deborah cried out from the force of his assault, but did not let go of her own cheeks. Her flesh was sinking a bit between her white knuckled fingers.

"Very good," Mr. Dean said in approval, grinding a bit against her bottom. Deborah was now stuffed in both cunt and ass, and felt completely packed.

Mr. Dean began a slow withdrawal from her ass, making her distended gate burn in agony; she felt like she was on fire. Tears streamed down her face. Still, she did not let go of her cheeks, but tried to pull them apart even farther, giving Mr. Dean more room, making it easier for him to ease in and out as he ravaged her asshole. After a few slow, even thrusts, he began to glide smoothly in and out of her ass, and the burning receded.

Although he had not moved this entire time, allowing Deborah to accustom herself to Mr. Dean's cock up her ass, Mr. Sinclaire's substantial prick was still hard inside her cunt. Now, he glanced at Mr. Dean, his eyes full of hidden meaning, and nodded.

Mr. Sinclaire unlocked Deborah from his tight hold, and pushed her up a bit off his chest--not enough to hinder Mr. Dean in any way from continuing his ramming, but enough to slide her up and down Mr. Sinclaire's own stiff cock. Deborah's eyes flared at the sudden jolt of pleasure.

The two men began to time their strokes, so that Mr. Dean withdrew his cock from Deborah's clinging ass just as Mr. Sinclaire lowered her down onto his own engorged prick; and then Mr. Dean would drive in, shoving his cock up her straining hole, while gliding her up Mr. Sinclaire's glistening member, until just the bulbous head remained inside.

Deborah was now being fucked in both cunt and ass, and pleasuring both men simultaneously; and was beginning to get quite carried away herself.

Soon, she was bouncing up and down on Mr. Sinclaire's wide frame, trying to cram more male meat inside her gaping pussy, as Mr. Dean rammed her from behind, jarring her thin body, shoving her up and down Mr. Sinclaire's long cock with driving force.

Both men tried to hold her steady as they pounded into her, and all Deborah could do was steady herself against Mr. Sinclaire's strong chest and hang on.

She could feel the first quiver of orgasm come from her impaled asshole, sucking in Mr. Dean's long length; her ass clenched in agonizing pleasure. Colors began to burst forth inside her head and under her eyelids like fireworks.

She came violently, yelling and lurching her whole body, writhing between both men as all her pelvic muscles seemed to constrict around both cocks.

And then the men were coming too, pulling her hips back and forth and straining against both her ravaged holes, Mr. Dean pumping into her spasming asshole as he erupted deep inside her rectum, Mr. Sinclaire lifting his hips completely as Deborah could actually feel his dick explode inside her pussy. Waves of bliss jolted her again, and again, and again, until she lay across Mr. Sinclaire's sweaty body, oblivious to anything but her own breathing and the feeling of the two depleted cocks quickly shrinking inside her.

Mr. Dean got out first, slowly pulling away until he was free of her clamping ass, which now seemed to want to trap him inside. He shuddered with the delicious feel of it, then fell onto the bed as her ass closed shut. Mr. Sinclaire lifted Deborah's limp body off his own, gently moved her over on his side, and sank back.

Together, the three of them slowly returned to earth, letting their sweaty skin cool down inside the soft silky mattress.

As her breath returned to normal, Deborah turned to look at Mr. Sinclaire: he had a hand laying across his face, breathing raggedly. She looked at Mr. Dean, who was gazing back at her with cloudy, half hooded eyes.

Looking at the two men who were still recovering from the pleasure they had wracked from her body, and feeling very, very proud of herself, Deborah threw back her head and chuckled in triumph.

Mark and Audra

MARK AND AUDRA MISSEL had been married for seven years. Childless by choice, they enjoyed their free and easy lifestyle, traveling often, visiting friends, and entertaining frequent guests with wild dinner parties.

Deeply committed to each other, what made them so compatible was the shared belief that monogamy was not necessary for a good marriage. He had his lovers, and so did she; and they would often trade partners with other couples who shared in their beliefs. Years ago, the Missels would have been labeled "swingers." But now, when pressed for an explanation, they stated simply that they had an open relationship.

Not that they didn't have rules. While sleeping with other people was acceptable, even expected, they had to be perfectly honest with each other about their opposite love partners. There could be no hidden trysts, no secret rendezvous taking place in the shadows. When Audra went out, she had to tell her husband exactly where she was going, and with whom; and the same was true for Mark. It was how they kept their marriage thriving: through absolute honesty and trust.

Audra, unfortunately, broke her husband's trust one month, by fucking a co-worker numerous times and failing to tell her husband about it. What initially confused her husband about the affair was that the co-worker happened to be a woman.

But the end result was the same: Audra had deceived him. She had been sleeping with her lover for weeks, yet had kept that simple fact from her husband. When Mark finally discovered his wife's deception, threats of divorce followed suit.

Audra had looked into marriage counselling. But what kind of therapist would understand their lifestyle? Their moral standards? And she was running out of time: Mark, unable to either forgive Audra or at least punish her for her sins, was already preparing to leave.

Then Audra had found the Hotel Bentmoore. Willing to try anything at that point, she scheduled their visit posthaste.

When they got the hotel, the front desk clerk noticed immediately how they regarded each other like strangers, cold and businesslike. After checking in, the couple ate together in the hotel dining room, but barely spoke to each other across the table. One would have thought they were strangers on a first date, a date going very badly.

Once the Missels returned upstairs, they changed for their scheduled "activity" in separate rooms, she in the bedroom and he in the bathroom; and when Mr. Brooks came to bring them below, Mark walked ahead, next to their liaison, while Audra trailed behind.

Mr. Brooks walked briskly to a door and pressed the button, letting their host know they had arrived; but when he opened the door, Audra was surprised to see that the room was small, and contained only three chairs. It looked more like a meeting room than anything else.

Mr. Dean was waiting for them. Unlike how he dressed within the confines of the activity rooms, he was now wearing a crisp white shirt tucked into his fitted slacks, buttoned all the way up to the neck. With his black hair combed impeccably back and his tailor-made clothes fitting him like second skin, he looked more like a business executive than a host of the Hotel Bentmoore.

Mr. Dean watched the way Mr. and Mrs. Missel entered the room, taking note of their lack of enthusiasm, the distance separating the two people, and the simmering rage and hurt behind Mr. Missel's eyes. He noticed the way Mrs. Missel would glance at her husband, her face full of longing, and then quickly look down.

"Let us sit for a minute," Mr. Dean said, motioning them to their seats. They sat awkwardly, facing one another other, yet not looking each other in the eyes.

"Now then--let's not waste any time. The two of you have come to the Hotel Bentmoore because of Audra's dishonesty and betrayal. You, Mr. Missel, cannot find a way to deal with it or move past it; you both need help to resolve your differences. Am I correct?"

"Yes," Audra whispered. Her husband nodded curtly. Mr. Dean leaned on his knees and steepled his fingers.

"Audra. Are you prepared to be completely honest with us both now, and tell us why you went behind your husband's back, despite the risk, knowing it would hurt him so badly?"

Audra took a shuddering breath and clasped her hands together. "I wanted to tell Mark about her--my coworker."

"The woman you slept with," Mr. Dean clarified.

"Yes. I'd been having feelings for her for a long time--I'd even been fantasizing about her. I just didn't know how to tell Mark." Mark looked at his wife in surprise, and, Mr. Dean noticed, with a stab of fear.

"When you say feelings...do you mean personal feelings? Something other than basic desire, carnal lust?" Mr. Dean asked her. "Do you now have an emotional attachment to this woman?"

"No, no, not at all," Audra said quickly. "I love my husband. I never wanted to hurt him."

"But you *did* hurt him. Why?"

"Because...I was afraid. I knew that if this was a man I wanted to sleep with, Mark wouldn't have had a problem with it. But if he found out it was a woman..." She glanced at her husband. "I was afraid he'd think differently of me."

Mr. Dean turned to Mark. "Is she right, Mark? Would you have thought differently of your wife if you found out she was fantasizing about a woman? You would have, perhaps, thought less of her?"

"Of course not!" Mr. Missel said. "I mean...I guess it would have taken me by surprise, certainly...and I would have needed some time to get used to the idea...but I wouldn't have thought *less* of her. You didn't give me enough credit, Audra," he said angrily, looking into his wife's face for the first time. "You should have told me about these feelings of yours, given me a chance to respond. You shouldn't have kept your fantasies from me, and you certainly shouldn't have gone behind my back."

Audra had tears running down her face. "I know. I'm so sorry, Mark." She let the tears fall, and could no longer look up.

Mr. Dean saw the way Audra's tears brought her husband anguish and dismay: Mark's face twisted up into a hard scowl as he kept himself from consoling his wife. It was obvious Mark wanted things to be right between them, the way it had been before, but he didn't know how to move past his wife's transgression.

"Mark," Mr. Dean said. "If Audra is punished, here, tonight, with my help...are you willing to accept your wife's punishment and put all this behind you? Can you move past her sins, start anew?"

"Yes," Mark said. "She should be punished for what she has done, but I don't trust myself to do it properly. But--I need to know she understands how badly she has hurt me, and shares my pain. I need to know she won't do it again."

Mr. Dean looked at Audra. "What about you, Audra? Are you willing to submit to my punishment, take everything I give you, and earn your husband's offer for a second chance?"

"Yes," she said softly. "Oh, yes. I'll do anything."

Mr. Dean smiled. "Then I see no reason to wait. Let's get this done right now," he said, and rose from his chair.

He opened the door to their small room, revealing their liaison, Mr. Brooks, waiting just outside. Mr. Brooks led the three of them to another door, and they marched through, with Audra in the rear; but this time, when she went through, she heard the door lock behind her.

Audra looked around, and a feeling of trepidation filled her. The spacious room was scattered with pieces of large, ominous looking equipment, with hooks and handles attached to each piece. One still had a piece of chain attached to it, dangling loosely to the floor, and hanging from the other end was a leather cuff, unbuckled but still bent in a narrow C shape; it didn't take much imagination to figure out what *that* was probably used for.

In the corner of the room was a wardrobe, double doored and slightly open; inside, hanging from the door, Audra caught a glimpse of a rod, a crop, and a cane. She quickly moved her eyes away to take in the rest of the room, and realized that, almost hidden inside the paint around the room, were hooks, set into walls and ceiling. She swallowed hard. Would she end up hanging from one of those hooks before the night was over?

Mr. Dean noticed Audra's rising fear and had some pity on her. The sooner they got started, the sooner it would be over. He would not go easy on her, of course. That would defeat the purpose of the activity.

He moved to the padded bench on the far side of the room, and beckoned the anxious woman over.

"Come here, Audra," he said. "It's time to face your punishment."

She eyed the bench, but did not move.

"Your husband will only forgive you if he sees you are repentant," Mr. Dean said simply.

Audra couldn't disagree with his logic, but suddenly the idea of walking freely to her own uncertain fate was too much for her, and her eyes filled with fear. Mr. Dean, seeing her panic, took pity on her again, and grabbed her by the hand to lead her to the bench. He could feel her hand shaking inside his own.

He left her by the bench for a moment to fetch some things from the wardrobe. When he came back, he was holding in his hands wrist cuffs and chains. Audra gasped. Mr. Dean looked at her resolutely; the time for pity was over.

"Hold out your hands to me, Audra," he ordered, his voice thick with authority. Audra turned to look at her husband for guidance or support, but Mr. Missel merely watched her, waiting to see if she would refuse.

"Hands, please, Audra," Mr. Dean repeated, more sternly this time.

Gulping, Audra held out her hands. One at a time, Mr. Dean attached the soft leather cuffs to each of her wrists. She lowered her hands to her sides, and the chains rattled on the floor. Mr. Dean gestured her over to the bench.

It was easy enough for Audra to get the idea what she had to do: she bent over it. The bench being long and slightly over waist high, she needed to push herself up a bit to bend at the waist, and once she was over, her legs hung straight down.

The bench was padded, and not *too* uncomfortable... but then Mr. Dean moved to the front of the bench, grabbed the chains attached to her wrist cuffs, and pulled her hands down, connecting the chains to hooks set into the floor. It was done so fast, Audra didn't have time to protest; and once it was done, she couldn't raise her arms at all. Instinctively, Audra tried to pull at the chains: she was quite effectively locked down.

Now Mr. Dean rolled up his sleeves and set about staging the rest of the room. He dragged a chair from across the room over to the bench, so that Mr. Missel could have a good view of his wife's upcoming punishment. He motioned Mr. Missel to have a seat, and Mr. Missel did so quickly, a twisted grin playing across his lips.

That done, Mr. Dean went back to the wardrobe and began to remove more objects from inside, placing them on a small wheeled tray. When he was satisfied with what he had on the tray, he pulled it along with him, back to where Audra was splayed across the bench. From her view, Audra could not see what was on the tray. But when she turned her head to the side, she could see her husband, and she knew the hot gleam in his eyes did not bode well for her.

"Let us start by getting you undressed," Mr. Dean said casually. "I hope you followed instructions, Audra. Otherwise I will be cutting *all* your clothes off you."

Audra swallowed hard. "I followed instructions, Sir."

"Good. With your permission, then....?" Mr. Dean was not asking Audra; he was asking her husband. Mark nodded.

Mr. Dean grabbed a pair of scissors off the tray and began to cut Audra's shirt off her. She felt the cold steel next her skin, moving up her back and arms, and bit her lip. Mr. Dean cut down the sleeves and back, pulling the material away from her once it was free.

Audra couldn't understand why she couldn't have taken off her shirt before being chained to the bench; but seeing the heat in her husband's eyes, she began to understand. He was enjoying seeing the clothes being cut away from her body.

Underneath the shirt she had donned a strapless, push up corset, hooked down the side. Mr. Dean got to work unhooking it, and had it expertly removed from her after only a few moments. He pulled the material out from under her; bent over the bench as she was, the two men could not see her breasts, but Audra was now naked from the waist up.

She thought her skirt would go next, but she was wrong. Mr. Dean had her step out of her shoes, crouching down to move them out of the way himself. And then Audra felt his hands on her legs; he was buckling cuffs around her ankles, too. She thought her ankles would next be chained to the floor. Again, she was wrong.

Mr. Dean went back to the wardrobe, and when he returned, he had in his hands a strange metal rod, about three feet wide.

"A spreader bar," Mr. Dean explained casually. He tapped Audra's ankles, motioning her to spread them, and she did as much as she could, straining against her skirt. Mr. Dean locked the bar in place between the Audra's ankle cuffs. Her legs were now locked to the bar, separated as they were; she could move them up and down, but could not close them. The sensation was jarring, to say the least.

But Mr. Dean was still not done: he looped another chain around the spreader bar and into a hook centered on the floor. Now Audra's legs were frozen in place: she couldn't close them, and she couldn't raise them more than a few inches off the floor.

Mr. Dean moved to her side, pondering the situation.

"I think we'll use the paddle," he said, looking down at her. "Just to warm things up."

Audra thought he would retrieve a paddle from the tray and begin to spank her skirted bottom. But she was wrong, and quickly decided that she ought to stop assuming she knew what was going to come next. Mr.

Dean obviously had complete control over the situation, while she was the one stretched over the bench; and she would only know what was going to happen to her as much as her punisher wanted her to know.

What he didn't let her know was that he was about to lift her skirt and uncover her ass.

Delicately, Mr. Dean began to raise Audra's skirt up, scrunching the material past her thighs, over her hips, and finally, around her waist, revealing the twin domes of her pantied ass to both males in the room.

He rolled the material a bit so it would stay in place, forming a ring around her midsection. Mr. Dean gave both himself and Mark a moment to gaze on Audra's smooth, rounded ass, curved lusciously and jutting out from the bench.

Audra squirmed under the eyes of the two men, or at least tried; she couldn't move that much. But watching her husband's reaction, noting his open look of attraction and the lust that clouded his eyes, she smiled. He had not looked at her like that for a long time.

But now Mr. Dean was taking things a step further: he was reaching up and hooking his fingers into her panties, and began to slowly pull them down. Inch by inch, her panties moved down her thighs, revealing her naked, creamy bottom to the eyes of both men.

She could not see Mr. Dean behind her, but she could see Mark, and he was taking long, shuddering breaths.

Mr. Dean didn't stop until he had pulled her panties all the way down, and they stretched across her spread knees.

With the spreader bar in place, Audra could not close her legs. Her ass crack was slightly spread open, revealing the hidden shadow between them and smoky pink skin. Between her legs, her bulging pussy lips remained closed, sticky from her feminine juices; but they were still prominently on display, and Audra knew she had no defense if Mr. Dean decided to make use of her vulnerable cunt as part of her punishment.

But Mr. Dean seemed satisfied with her bare ass, at least for now.

"I think this will do," he said.

Now he went back to the tray to retrieve the paddle. When he returned, he took position next to Audra's bent form, looked at Mark, and asked pointedly, "Shall we begin?"

Mark nodded. Audra closed her eyes.

The first strike of the paddle hit her right across the bottom crescent of her left cheek, and Audra yelped.

"Now, Audra," Mr. Dean said sternly. "That was only a light tap. You must learn to take your punishment with better control." He struck again. Audra yelped once more.

"Really, Audra, if you do not stop, I will have to gag you for this part of the punishment," Mr. Dean warned her. This time, when he struck, Audra hissed through her teeth, but didn't cry out. "There's a good girl," Mr. Dean said.

He began to pepper her ass with hard, flat smacks of the paddle, alternating between cheeks, spreading the blows around a bit so that her bottom would blush evenly from thigh to thigh.

Through it all, Audra was careful never to make a sound, save for a sharp intake of breath now and then. But from across the bench, she watched the excitement grow in her husband's eyes, and knew he was getting extremely turned on, seeing his wife getting spanked by their host.

When a rosy pink glow began to blush across her entire ass, Mr. Dean stopped and held the paddle out.

"Come here, Mark," he said. "You should participate in this, too."

Mark rose awkwardly; there was a definite bulge in his pants, making it difficult to walk.

"What do I do?" He asked.

"Spank your wife," Mr. Dean replied. "Let her know how displeased you are with her behavior."

Mark took the paddle from Mr. Dean and stepped to Audra's side. He gazed upon his chained wife, her jutting ass, and smooth, sloping back. He couldn't help it: with a single hand he gingery felt up Audra's fiery ass, and got a whimper from his wife in response. Despite his soft touch, his rough hand caressing her ass felt like bristles against her skin, and at that point Audra was hoping for some leniency from her husband. But she was about to be disappointed, for Mark pressed his hand in even harder against her flesh, moving it in a circular motion and making Audra moan.

Mark gripped the paddle in his hand, raised it high, and let it swing down on Audra's cringing ass, striking it right across her crack. This time, Audra yelled loudly, and Mark watched in fascination as she squeezed her butt cheeks together, trying to cringe away from the sting.

He smacked her again, and again, and again, unhindered by his wife's cries or her struggles against the chains.

"You deserve this, Audra," he said sadly between smacks. "You need to learn your lesson."

Ignoring her pleas and assurances that she would never do it again, he kept up the spanking, until his wrist began to hurt and the anger had left him completely. To his surprise, his anger had been replaced by overwhelming lust, a heady desire to fuck his wife's pussy right then and there.

He looked down at his handiwork: Audra's butt was now even redder than before. It looked burned, a shiny glowing crimson that made even him wince a little to see it. But he felt good, better than he'd felt since he had discovered Audra's betrayal, and he staggered back to the chair.

He collapsed onto it, breathing hard. His cock strained against his pants, bulging against the zipper, and he shifted around in the chair.

Thinking the ordeal over, Audra rested into the bench padding, breathing hard herself.

"We are not done," Mr. Dean announced. The couple both looked at him in surprise. "What Audra did was a serious offense against your shared bond, your mutual trust. Her punishment must be matching in severity if the two of you are to remember it with the proper perspective and appreciation."

With that, Mr. Dean went back to the tray, and took from it a strange, brownish, bumpy...thing. Mark and Audra had once taken a cooking class together, and they both knew the thing for what it was: a large, raw, ginger root.

One long knobby end of the root had been shaved, revealing the hard yellowish meat inside. The end of the root had been sculpted, as well, forming a wide, smooth, and rather long rod. A narrow notch had been carved out around the base of the sculpted root.

Mr. Dean admired the root for a moment, smiling ominously at his handy work. Then he held it up in front of Audra's face.

"Do you know what this is?"

"Yes, it's a ginger root."

"Yes. Do you know what it's used for, besides cooking?"

Audra swallowed. "No."

"It goes up the ass. It burns like hell. Tell me, Audra, have you ever taken anything up the ass before? Perhaps engaged a bit in anal play?"

"No, never," she said, her voice hoarse.

Mr. Dean looked contrite. "Well, then, I'm sorry your first experience is going to have to be so painful. Let me just tell you that anal play can be fun, and can help you reach intense orgasms...don't let this deter you, should you want to try it at a later date. But tonight, Audra... tonight, pleasure is not on the docket."

Mr. Dean rose and offered the ginger to her husband.

"Mark, would you like to do the honor of sticking this up your wife's ass?"

Mark shook his head no, but made no protest as Mr. Dean stepped behind his wife.

"Now wait--" Audra spluttered. Mr. Dean stopped.

"Are you willing to take your punishment, Audra? Or do you refuse?" Mr. Dean waited. Audra looked at Mark, who was watching her with furrowed brows, the bulge in his lap becoming a tent beneath his pants. She squeezed her eyes shut.

"Very well," she said. "I'll take it."

Mr. Dean stepped behind her, and with one hand, began to splay apart her ass cheeks. Audra moaned. She could feel the crease between her smooth domes widening, revealing her smoky valley inside, and right in the center, the cringing ring of her tightening asshole. Instinctively, she tried to squeeze her butt cheeks together, hiding it away from prying eyes; but Mr. Dean held her open with stubborn fingers.

In fact, he gestured Mark to move closer, so Mark could get a better view of his wife's cringing bottom, and what their host was about to do to it.

Mr. Dean took aim with the ginger root.

"With anal toys, it is polite to lubricate them first, ease them in," he said, talking under his breath as if making light commentary. "But the ginger must have full-on contact with the skin. Lubricant of any kind would hinder the effect."

He pointed the blunted tip of the root to Audra's shrinking rectum, and Audra took a sharp intake of breath.

"Here we go," Mr. Dean said, and pushed in the root.

"Angh," Audra grunted, feeling her sphincter widen under the sudden assault. "Ungh--oh--" She tried to push herself forward into the bench padding, away from the ginger root now poking into her ass. But there was no getting away from it, spread and chained as she was.

Mr. Dean pushed it in gradually, letting her get accommodated as much as she could to the strange sensation of the slick hard root impaling her up the ass. But he never pulled back, and never stopped; and slowly, the root began to stretch her straining asshole, slipping in farther and higher. Audra's husband watched, enthralled, as the root dully disappeared up his wife's elegant, virgin bottom.

Mr. Dean kept pressing, getting grunts and whimpers from the chained woman, until the very widest part pushed through her straining gate. The notch slipped tightly into the rim of Audra's sensitive hole, neatly plugging her spasming ass.

Once the ginger root was in place, Mr. Dean let go her of her butt cheeks, letting them close around the rest of the knobby ginger root, and stepped away from Audra's proffered behind to wait.

They didn't have to wait long.

"Oh--oh--OH--OH God--Ahhhh--" The burning juice of the ginger began to soak into Audra's delicate tissues, making her twist her hips; the chain locking her legs and the spreader bar to the floor rattled and clanged. Audra squeezed her eyes shut, and her face contorted in agony.

"Oh Lord--Oh dear Jesus--OH GOD--" Her voice rose in perfect correlation to the pain coming from her stretched, straining hole. Her plugged sphincter squeezed and cringed reflexively, and every time it did, the burning juices of the devilish root hurt her even more. Sweat beaded across her forehead and back.

"OH MY GOD!" Audry was struggling hard now, trying to squeeze her legs together, pulling against her bonds. But there was no expelling the root, the notched end made sure of that, and the burning ache coming from her tight plugged hole worsened only further. Tears began to run down her cheeks. She started to yell and holler.

Mark rose from his chair in alarm, looking at Mr. Dean; but Mr. Dean shook his head silently, and Mark sank slowly back into his chair. Unmindful of her husband's reaction, Audra continued to plead and yell, bucking her hips and pulling against her bonds. The sweat ran down her body.

As Audra flailed, Mr. Dean went back to the tray; and then, to Mark's shock, he returned with a long, thin, and vicious looking whip. As Mark watched, Mr. Dean took position behind Audra's plugged bottom, and began to whip his wife's ass.

WIP--WIP--WIP--

The light but stinging whip cut lines across the red glow of Audra's ass, biting deep; and every time it did, Audra clenched her rear cheeks in pain, tightening the grip of her clenching asshole around the ginger root.

"AHH!" She shrieked, and arched up. Mr. Dean waited until the cut of the whip receded against the burning agony coming from her ass; but as soon as it did, and Audra bent back down in a vain attempt to relax and dilate her throbbing sphincter away from the root, Mr. Dean would whip her again, so that there was no let up from the pain.

The whip hurt, but nothing like the pure, white hot agony coming from the ginger root stuffed up her rear hole, and Mr. Dean made sure she kept that ginger root tight up her bottom.

She began to beg.

"Please, Mark, please, oh God PLEASE--" She was crying now, the sobs catching in her voice as she pleaded with her husband for mercy.

WIP--WIP--WIP--

"PLEASE, MARK, PLEASE!"

WIP--WIP--WIP--

Finally, Mr. Missel could take no more, and rose from the chair to stop the whip from falling across his wife's gleaming butt again.

"I think that's enough," he said softly. Audra's sobbing was loud and anguished, and tore at his heart. "She's learned her lesson."

"Very well," Mr. Dean said, nodding. He balanced the whip back down on the tray and moved away. Mr. Missel took position behind Audra's ass and slowly opened her rear cheeks, getting a good look at the glowing, striped domes and the ginger root stuffed between them.

To his surprise, Audra's pussy was shining with her juices: she was incredibly wet. She was swollen as well, engorged from the blood pumping through her pelvic region. Mark wanted nothing more than to yank down his pants and drive his own engorged cock straight into his wife's warm, wet pussy, but pushed the thought away.

Instead, he held Audra's cheeks apart with one hand, and slowly, began the delicate job of pulling out the ginger root.

"OOH--" Audra moaned. As the root slid out, rubbing against her burning rim, her voice rose in pitch. But once the widest part was out and the root began to narrow, Audra could feel her asshole clenching shut, and she groaned in relief.

The root now out, she collapsed against the padding and took long, shuddering breaths. Sweat coated her skin, making the bench feel slick beneath her.

Mr. Dean moved inconspicuously to a corner of the room as Mark began the slow task of unbuckling his wife from the bench, pulling away her bonds one cuff at a time. At last, when she was free, he pulled her up, and held her to his chest.

"It's okay, it's over now, shh, baby, sweetheart, it's all over--" Audra began to cry against his chest. Mark leaned against the bench and held her, rocking her back and forth a bit as she clung to him. Audra was half naked, her skirt down but her panties still around her knees; she looked ragged and pathetic.

"Audra, honey, it's done now," he said, petting and soothing his sweet and vulnerable wife. She cried for another few minutes; then her breath began to even out, jolted now and then with a hiccuped sob, and she began to calm down. And all the while, Mark continued to hold and rock her, hugging her to him like a child.

"I'm sorry, Mark," Audra whispered into his shirt. "I'm so, so sorry for the way I hurt you." Her lip quivered, and another sob shook her sweaty frame.

"I forgive you," Mark said against her hair. "I love you and forgive you, Audra. So let's make a fresh start from here on in, okay?" Audra looked up, and smiled brightly when she saw the sincerity in her husband's eyes.

"Thank you, Mark. I love you so much." She hugged him tightly, snuggling into his chest. Mr. Dean gave them another few minutes before he cleared his throat.

"I think that's enough for tonight," he said, handing Mark Audra's corset. He diplomatically turned away as Audra pulled away from her husband just enough to get dressed.

Audra's cut up shirt would be left behind, of course, but the corset would cover her enough to get her back to their room. In the last minute, Audra decided to leave her panties behind, too. They hurt too much, rubbing against her bottom.

The burn from her ravaged asshole wasn't as bad as before, but it still throbbed, making the whole area pulse. The sensation was unexpected, and somewhat disconcerting.

Once Audra was as dressed as she was going to be, Mr. Dean pressed the button to call for Mr. Brooks, and turned to the hugging couple.

"Tomorrow...shall we say same time?"

Audra and Mark looked at each other, then back at their host in confusion.

"Audra's punishment is done," Mark said. "I've forgiven her. I thought we're finished."

"Audra's been punished, but I think there are still a few issues that need to be resolved," Mr. Dean replied. "And I think it would be best for the two of you to deal with them now, while you're still at the hotel. But if you prefer to go home tomorrow...."

Mark looked questioningly at Audra, and Audra nodded her head in agreement. "We will come back tomorrow," Mark said. "Same time."

"Good," Mr. Dean said. At that moment, Mr. Brooks opened the door, and the three of them parted ways, with Audra pulling her husband out of the room quickly. Mark let his wife drag him along, looking after her in surprise at her sudden urgency.

Mr. Dean smiled, watching the couple disappear into the elevator. He knew they were about to have a very pleasant evening upstairs in their bedroom--especially Mr. Missel. The aftereffects of the ginger root would see to that.

It would leave Audra's whole pelvic area engorged and tingly, leaving her with a maddening itch, an intense need for sexual release, that only a stiff cock pumping into her throbbing cunt could provide.

Mr. Missel would soon be very happy to relieve his needy wife.

*****

The next day, the satisfied couple returned to Mr. Dean to submit once more to his tutelage and guidance. Only this time, they walked into their activity room hand in hand, smiling at each other as their host stepped forward from the corner of the room.

But today, Mr. Dean was not alone. A woman stood behind him, remaining slightly in the shadows, as their host walked towards them. She leaned languidly back against the wall, eyeing them both with half hooded eyes, perfectly comfortable in her almost nude pose.

Wearing only a pair of sheer nylon panties and a translucent brassiere, her long straight blond hair was pulled back in a ponytail, but her bangs cut across her forehead in a sharp, straight line, right over her eyes, highlighting her high cheekbones and delicate jaw. With swooping lashes and thick lips, she did not exactly fit the standard of what could be called beautiful, but was instead incredibly sultry and erotic, and both Mr. and Mrs. Missel could feel their bodies reacting to her slender, mouth watering body.

"This is one of my associates, here at the Hotel Bentmoore," Mr. Dean said. "I have asked her to join us for tonight, if you are willing. But let us sit, and I'll explain to you why I've asked her here."

Instead of grabbing separate lounge chairs, Mr. and Mrs. Missel sat next to each other on the edge of the large four poster bed taking up the entire corner of the spacious room. Mr. Dean passed them a flitting smile before slipping back into his usual serious countenance. He grabbed a chair, and sat across from them both.

"The two of you originally came to the hotel for help, to deal with Audra's betrayal," he said. "You needed to find a way to move beyond it." The couple on the bed both nodded. "But, as awful as she behaved, Audra is not the only one to blame here. You, Mark, helped to create an environment that forced Audra to question your feelings for her."

Audra's eyes widened, while Mark began to splutter in protest. Mr. Dean put up his hand to stop him.

"Hear me out, Mark. You said yourself yesterday, you admitted it, it would have taken you by surprise to hear about your wife's fantasies to fuck another woman. You would have needed some time to get used to the idea, you said. Now why is that?"

"Because Audra's not a *lesbian*," Mark said, taken aback. "She has sex with men. We are both *straight*. If she starts sleeping with women, then...."

"Then, what? She is not the person you thought you married? She is someone else, someone you can't be with anymore?" Audra looked intently at her husband, while Mark opened his mouth in surprise. But then he shrugged, unable to think of an acceptable response, and Audra looked down, forlorn.

"Mark, there is nothing wrong with Audra finding another woman attractive," Mr. Dean said. "It shouldn't change the way you see her in any way. In fact, you need to realize that there is probably more to Audra than you have ever realized, and tapping into her fantasies might just bring the two of you closer together. It might make both of you more satisfied in your relationship." Mark raised his eyes in surprise, while Audra looked hopeful.

"But Mark...you need to see exactly what Audra wanted so badly that she was willing to deceive you and go behind your back to get it. And Audra--you need to be willing to let go, show Mark your secrets and reveal everything to him, what you've been fantasizing about for so long." He paused, letting the truth of his words sink in. "Are the two of you willing to take this to the next level? Face what you've both been too afraid to reveal?"

Mark and Audra squirmed and looked at each other uncomfortably, but they both nodded.

"Very good," their host said. "In that case, Mark--if you would have a seat."

He motioned Mark over to a padded chair facing the bed, and Mark walked over to it, shifting his weight as he sat down to get comfortable. But he was surprised when he looked up, and saw Mr. Dean coming towards him with wrist cuffs.

"Now what--"

"You are to be a spectator only tonight, Mark--you may not join in the activity in any way. You may not get up, you may not go to you wife...and most importantly, you may not touch yourself, either. You need to experience some of the frustration Audra must have been suffering all this time by being forced to hold herself back, deny herself her fantasies, in fear of losing you."

While both Audra and Mark looked on, Mr. Dean cuffed Mark's wrists and buckled them to the chair.

By the time Mr. Dean was done, Mark could twist his arms a little bit inside the cuffs, but not much. Audra sat on the bed, watching her husband get shackled to the chair...thinking, in the back of her mind, that he deserved a little discomfort, after what she'd been put through the night before.

Mr. Dean now beckoned to the woman waiting in the shadows, who padded over to them on slightly tiptoed feet.

"Now then. This is Judy...I have asked her to join Audra in the activity for tonight."

Audra gasped. Mark twisted his head with a stern look on his face, watching this new addition to their little drama go directly to his wife without offering him so much as a wayward glance.

With an easy gait, Judy walked over to Audra on the bed. She stopped when her legs hit Audra's knees, and stood before the sitting woman in proud glory. Then, she reached down, took both of Audra's hands in her own, and brought them to her mouth, kissing each one with soft lips as she gazed into Audra's eyes.

Audra didn't pull her hands away, but squeezed Judy's hands softly. Judy began to graze her lips back and forth across Audra's knuckles. The wanton look in her eyes made Audra's toes curl.

Judy pulled Audra to her feet, and slowly, with fluid movements, she tilted her head, and kissed Audra full on the mouth.

Mark tried to rise from his chair. "Now hold on here--Audra--"

"What is the problem, Mark?" Mr. Dean asked dryly from his place in the corner. Mark stopped his struggles against the chair.

"She can't just kiss my wife--"

"Would you rather she be kissing you?"

Mark clenched his jaw, while Mr. Dean looked at him wryly.

"Would you not like to trade places with your wife? Wouldn't you be kissing Judy's sweet lips right now if you could?....Why would you deny Audra the pleasure?"

Mark didn't answer, but his eyes glared mutinously at his wife. She stepped away from Judy and looked down.

Mr. Dean frowned. "Mark, I must insist that you remain quiet," he ordered. "And if you cannot follow such a simple instruction, I will gag you."

"But--"

"Quiet!" Mr. Dean roared. Mark shut up.

Judy, who had turned to watch the byplay between host and husband, now cast her eyes back to Audra and reached for her. Audra looked anxious, but let herself be pulled into the other woman's embrace. When she was close enough to rub against Judy's breasts, the experienced hostess leaned in to kiss her once more.

After her husband's objection, it took Audra a moment to relax, and respond; but soon, her eyes closed and her mouth opened, and the two women were kissing each passionately, letting their tongues roam into each other's mouths. They remained locked together for quite a few moments, enjoying the tantalizing embrace, as their tongues and hands roamed.

After a few minutes, Judy broke away, and looked questioningly at Mr. Dean.

"By all means, my dear," he said, sweeping his arm forward. "This is your show tonight."

Judy smiled, and turned back to Audra, who was breathing heavily and looking at her with half hooded eyes. Judy began to kiss Audra's neck, nibbling as she moved down the soft skin, leaving a trail of warm wetness and tingles. Audra closed her eyes and tilted her head, giving the woman better access.

As Judy continued her slow, leisurely kisses, she began to open Audra's blouse, working the buttons with nimble fingers. As soon as the top was opened, Judy moved her mouth in a downward path, tasting Audra's ample cleavage. Then, in one quick movement, she pulled Audra's shirt down her arms and flung it to the floor.

Audra arched back, her breasts heaving forward prominently inside her bra. Judy kissed the tops of her breasts, cupping them over the straining material; then, she reached behind and unclasped Audra's bra, letting it fall to the floor.

The two women both gasped as it fell to the ground, revealing Audra's creamy ample breasts, the crinkled aureoles, and the swelling, dark pink nipples. Without missing a beat, Judy tilted her head and took one of Audra's puckered nipples into her mouth.

"Oh!" Audra staggered back onto the bed, losing all strength in her legs; and Judy went with her, covering the shuddering woman with her own sleek body, never letting go of the hard, swollen nipple in her mouth. She sucked greedily, stabbing the highly sensitive skin with her tongue, getting a long moan of pleasure from her love partner.

After a few blissful moments, she released the distended nipple, only to claim the other with her demanding lips, making sucking noises with her soft, wonderful mouth.

Mark, meanwhile, was watching the pair intently, unable to look away. At first, he had been uncomfortable watching his wife being kissed and touched by another woman...but now, he was enthralled, captivated by the sight of his horny wife being serviced by the expert mouth of their hostess.

Judy picked her head up from Audra's proud breasts, and for a moment, Audra's eyes cleared. She smiled, and Judy smiled back; and then, with a knowing grin, Audra unclasped and pulled away Judy's bra, letting the woman's heavy breasts fall into her face.

Audra pushed her cheeks between the sweet smelling flesh, snuggling in; and then it was her turn to take the other woman's nipple into her mouth, giving back the same pleasure she had received moments ago. Judy groaned.

Soon, both women were on their sides across the bed, kissing and fondling each other, and Mark was having a hard time keeping still in his seat. His cock was now fully erect, pressing forcefully against his pants; he shifted this way and that, but being shackled as he was, he couldn't use his hands to maneuver things around. It was irritating, to the point of being almost painful.

Judy, meanwhile, had begun a slow exploration of Audra's belly with her tongue. Audra lay back, lost in her bliss, furrowing her brows now and then as her hostess moved ever lower. When Judy got the hem of Audra's skirt, she unzipped it, and lazily began to pull it, along with Audra's underpants, down her legs.

Without a whisper of protest, Audra let the other woman undress her completely. She seemed to be waiting now, giving Judy expectant looks as she squeezed the sheets in her hands. Judy smiled in understanding; then, moving gracefully, she maneuvered herself between Audra's legs.

Audra accommodated the curvaceous woman, spreading her legs wide. Judy shifted her weight downward, placing a hand on each of Audra's inner thighs to hold them apart; and then, with a smile, she dipped her head down, and touched her lips to Audra's pussy.

Audra arched back and let out a groan, widening her legs even further. Judy kissed Audra's labia, swollen with need, and ran her tongue teasingly up the crease separating the lips of her cunt. Audra inhaled sharply.

Slowly, Judy opened Audra's soft pink folds, pulling them lightly away, taking her time. Audra watched her with cloudy eyes, looking down at the face implanted between her legs. When Judy found her target, she poked out her tongue, and gently, she slid it in, right over Audra's nerve-filled clitoris.

Audra whooped. The jolt of pleasure she felt from Judy's brazen tongue was electrifying, and she twisted in the sheets. But Judy steadied her hands inside Audra's thighs, keeping them still as she continued to lap at the other woman's clitoris, widening her tongue and using long, hard strokes.

Audra didn't notice her husband's discomfort; she was too deep in her own carnal delight, mindless from the blissful feelings the other woman's velvety tongue were evoking, as it circled and danced, paying homage to Audra's throbbing clitoris.

But Mark was no longer so comfortable. He was pulling against the cuffs, gripping the chair handles tightly. Sweat began to pour from his face. His hips were bucking in the chair, making it tip and hop.

His cock felt huge inside his pants, ready to explode, and all he wanted to do now was throw himself on his wife laying languidly on the bed and ram his cock into her wet, gaping pussy. But he could not--he couldn't even touch himself.

His balls constricted, and his prick twitched and danced, begging for release. He could feel a wet spot where some pre-cum was already dripping from his prick hole.

He groaned, but said nothing; he was too afraid. The last thing he wanted now was for Mr. Dean to stop him from watching his wife's pussy being licked and sucked by their beautiful, willing hostess.

Judy kept up her licking, moving her lips now and then around Audra's folds to suck and kiss different pleasure points. And whenever she did so, Audra arched back in the sheets, tensing up every sinew in her body.

With a daring look in her eyes, Judy slipped two fingers up Audra's wet cunt, shoving hard.

"Uhh!" Audra's eyes flared. She thrust her hips up. Judy wiggled her fingers, and Audra gasped like a dying fish.

Feeling bold, Judy tried to stuff more fingers into Audra's stretching, spasming cunt. Audra scrunched up her face but didn't pull away. When the widest part of her hand slid snugly against Audra's pelvic bone, Judy stopped, and began a slow grind with her hand against Judy's pelvis, back and forth, in and out.

"Oh, oh, oh--" Audra was getting hit by waves of pleasure now, slamming into her body every time Audra's hand thrust in and wiggled. She spread her legs as wide as she could, and held onto the sheets with tight fists, gasping for air.

With her hand still deep inside Audra's hungry pussy, Judy sucked on her guest's clit, pressing lightly down with her satiny tongue and twisting it against the sensitive tissue again, and again, and again.

Audra began to make high pitched keening noises. Every time Judy thrusted and grinded her hand in, another jolt of pleasure ran through her like a live wire, and she convulsed from the exquisite thrill of it.

With one hand still firmly lodged up Audra's cunt, Judy slid her other hand up Audra's lithe body, and began to pinch her upstanding nipples, giving them each a short squeeze. She began to harmonize her tongue and hand thrusts; like a sexual concertist, she conducted the speed and rhythm of her movements, bringing Audra to the climax of their shared rhapsody.

"Oh Jesus, oh god...yes! Oh, yes!" The orgasm exploded from Audra's throbbing clit, radiating out of her pelvis and wracking her whole body. Judy kept thrusting and licking until she was sure Audra was done, waited until the convulsing woman had quieted down, and then she carefully pulled her hand away and lifted her glistening lips from Audra's slick pussy.

Audra lay back in the sheets, damp with sweat, and panting heavily. Judy, her work finished, stood up and padded to the back of the room with the grace of a sleek cat.

"Jesus. Jesus, Audra."

With a tranquil expression, Audra turned to her husband, and saw for the first time the effect her steamy love scene had had on him. His cock strained obscenely against his pants, trying to position itself straight up; it was obviously causing him some pain. Sweat was pouring down his face, and the tendons in his head and neck looked like they were about to explode. Mark shifted in his seat and twisted his wrists in the tight cuffs.

Audra smiled at him in satisfaction.

Mr. Dean stepped forward and looked at Mark, who was desperate to be out of the tortuous chair.

"What do you think now?" Mr. Dean asked. "Still think there's something wrong with your wife for wanting another woman to go down on her, eat out her pussy, make her come?"

"No. God, no," Mark said in a throaty whisper. "That was...that was..." his voice trailed away and he swallowed hard.

"Good," Mr. Dean said. He walked over to the bed and gave Audra a hand up. She wobbled a bit as she stood; she still felt weak from her intense orgasm. But after a couple moments, she had collected herself, and began to get dressed.

As she did, Mr. Dean unlocked Mark from the chair. As soon as Mark was free, he stood up and pushed a hand down into his pants, trying to get his painful erection under control.

By the time Mr. Brooks had been summoned and opened their door, Mr. Missel was more than ready to drag his wife back to their room and fuck her soundly. He wanted to hear her make the same high pitched keening cries she had made for Judy; he wanted to see the same lusty looks in her eyes.

Audra walked slightly more at ease, of course, having had her needs already met by the expert lips and fingers of their mysterious hostess; but she was reacting to her husband's incredible sexual need, too. Mr. Dean knew she would soon be just as frenzied as her husband to have Mark's engorged cock well up her already pre-moistened cunt.

Mr. Dean smiled as he watched the happy, horny couple leave the room without so much as a goodbye to their host.

"Think they'll be back?" Judy asked. She had not donned her bra, but was still wearing her panties, and Mr. Dean noticed that a circular wet stain had spread inside the crotch of the thin material.

"They'll be back, but not for my services," he said casually. "Maybe for yours, though."

"I won't mind. The wife's gorgeous, and she tastes great." She tilted her head, thinking. "The husband's pretty good looking, too."

"True," Mr. Dean sighed. He let his eyes linger on Judy's wet panties. "Tell me, Judy, do you have any other activities planned for tonight?"

"No, my schedule is free," she said. Her eyebrows furrowed as she took in his suddenly wolfish look. "Why?"

"Our guests were not the only ones turned on by your expert talent. I know I was--and by the looks of it, I think you were pretty turned on, too." He grabbed her by the hand and pushed her onto the bed. Judy squealed.

"I think an activity of our own is in order," he said, shoving up her legs and pulling off her underpants. Looking as serious as he always did, Mr. Dean lowered his head between her legs, and let his face disappear into her wet, warm cunt.

Judy, it turned out, was not the only one with an expert tongue. Mr. Dean had his talents, too.

Elizabeth

ELIZABETH WEBER WAS A young, wealthy, and beautiful socialite. At nineteen years old, her passport was already a haphazard puzzle booklet of stamps from different countries, and she knew first hand the smoky interiors of countless VIP rooms and secret clubs around the world. With her looks and her money, she was quickly waved through every door, welcomed into any circle.

She was also a brat.

When she was younger, most of her life had alternated between boarding school and skiing trips with her wealthier friends. But she was older now, out of school, away from anything that could even pass as discipline, and having a bit too much wild fun with her freedom. Her father didn't care what she did, as long she kept herself out of prison and away from the prying eyes of the paparazzi. It fell upon her stepmother to take an interest in what befell the newly blossomed woman, who was quickly becoming a hoyden.

Luckily, Elizabeth's stepmother soon grasped the real underlying problem plaguing the young woman, and found a way to convince Elizabeth to spend her upcoming weekend at the Hotel Bentmoore.

Of course, the convincing had to involve some insinuating mention of Elizabeth's rather large allowance, not to mention a few veiled threats from her father; but the discussion went civilly enough, and Elizabeth was soon on her way to the hotel.

When Mr. Shern met Elizabeth for the first time, he had her brought to him in one of the downstairs activity rooms as soon as she arrived. He was immediately taken with her careful dress and haughty attitude: she wore a short silk dress, royal blue, that dipped at her cleavage and showed off her small, pear shaped breasts most becomingly. The dress contrasted perfectly with her bright yellow, round-toed high heeled shoes, and the yellow ribbon tying up her long, strawberry blond hair looked modish in her tresses. The girl looked more like she was ready for a smoke and coffee at a London art club than a randy activity at the Hotel Bentmoore.

She eyed him speculatively, curious but without an ounce of fear. She didn't seem anxious at all, not now as Mr. Shern looked her over boldly (and he was only half dressed), and not before, when she had obviously heard the liaison shut the door behind her, effectively locking her in.

But Mr. Shern has spoken to Elizabeth's step-mother at length, and he knew what was probably going on in her head right now. He knew just how to handle a girl like this.

"Elizabeth, I am Mr. Shern. I will be your host during your visit to the Hotel Bentmoore," he said in a low, even voice. Elizabeth crossed her arms.

"That's nice," she replied. Mr. Shern smiled at her insolence. She was trying to act like she didn't care what he was saying, that it didn't even concern her. She would also try to challenge him every chance she could, at first. But she was smart; she would learn quickly.

"Your stepmother seems to think you need some... guidance, shall we say? From an older man. Someone who can steer you in the right direction, teach you a few things that will help you. Do you agree?"

"Does it matter?" Elizabeth retorted. "I'm here because I was bribed and blackmailed by my father. Three days, three fucking days I have to spend here, but then I'm gone. So why don't you teach me whatever you think you'll be able to fit in the next, oh, sixty hours, and then I can go." She tilted her head and thrust her hip to the side, letting him know exactly what she thought of his opinions.

But Mr. Shern was not to be pushed into anger. He had vast experience dealing with impudent little brats like her, and instead of showing her exactly how much her disrespect got to him, he sighed.

"You're right, three days will hardly be enough time to teach you anything. I doubt you'll learn much." She gasped, and Mr. Shern smiled in satisfaction. "But we'll see if we can manage to get a few things through your head, won't we?" Elizabeth opened her mouth to say something, but shut it quickly. She seemed unsure of herself now, and glanced at the door, weighing her options for a dignified escape. It was, of course, far too late for that.

Mr. Shern motioned her over to a chair. "Sit down, Elizabeth. Let's talk plainly, set some ground rules. I think we'll need to do that first off, if things are to go smoothly between us." Elizabeth made no move toward the chair. Mr. Shern regarded her sternly.

"For the duration of your stay, I will be teaching you what I think you need to learn to improve your life, and I will do this with or without your cooperation, Elizabeth. I only want you to understand what I expect, so things might go easier between us. But really, I don't care how you feel about the next few days. You can make your time in this room go by pleasantly, or you can make it hard on yourself. It's completely up to you." Elizabeth thought for a moment, then slowly, as if to show him she did it merely of her own accord, she sat down in the chair.

"Very good," Mr. Shern said. He took the chair opposite her and rested his elbows on his knees. "Now then. In this room, you will call me Sir. I am your host, I guide you in whatever activity I want you to engage in, and you will follow my orders immediately. You will comply obediently, like a good girl, or you will suffer the consequences. Do you understand?"

"Yes, Sir," she replied mulishly. Of course, she didn't understand, not really, and when the full gravity of his words finally hit her, Mr. Shern knew he would have a fight on his hands. But he was prepared for that, too.

"Now then...I need you to answer a few questions. Nothing that will get back to your father or stepmother, nothing that will ever leave this room. But I need you to answer truthfully, and I warn you young lady, I'm a pretty good at figuring out when I'm being lied to. So: how many men have you fucked?"

The vulgarity of the question shocked her, but she recovered quickly, and tried to be flippant with her answer to show her worldliness. "You mean fooled around with, or actually let penetrate me?"

"I mean actual penetration, and in case you were going to ask, I mean pussy, not ass." Elizabeth was taken aback. It had not even occurred to her he might mean *that*. She had never let anyone *near* her ass before.

"Too many to remember," she said, rallying once more. Mr. Shern's eyes furrowed.

"Try again."

"Really, I don't know."

"Try again."

"I don't understand what this has to do with anything," she snapped, glaring at him.

"Try again. And this time, I want a number, or there will be consequences."

She looked down into her lap. "Two," she said, and looked at him mutinously. "It's only been two, alright? I'm not this experienced, knowledgeable woman that everyone thinks I am. So what?"

"So what, indeed. There is nothing wrong with that number one way or the other; I simply wanted to know. Did you sleep with these boys many times?"

"No," she snapped. "They were one time hook-ups. Fuck them and forget about it. No expectations, no regrets."

"I'm sure that's what they told you," Mr. Shern murmured. "I wonder if it's true, though. Were they your age?"

"About."

"Where were these hook-ups?"

"At parties."

"At your home?"

"No, other people's homes. My friends."

"Did you orgasm?"

The question caught her completely off guard. "Well of course I...I...finished! I'm experienced enough for that!" She laughed, but it sounded forced.

"You're lying." Mr. Shern sat back in his chair and crossed his arms.

"No, I'm not. I came each time. It was amazing!" With her eyes, Elizabeth dared him to contradict her.

"Elizabeth, you're lying, and if you don't give me a straight answer right now, you're going to have to deal with some of those consequences I was talking about."

Elizabeth shot out of her chair. "Fine! Don't believe me! What are you going to do to me, huh? Tell my stepmom I didn't behave? Tell my dad? He doesn't care, you know. You just go ahead, try it." Her eyes were stormy, clear blue pools, and Mr. Shern caught a glimpse of the little girl inside, testing her boundaries, trying to find a hand that would hold her back from going too far. She was used to finding none. Well, Mr. Shern was about to show her how strong his hand could be.

He grabbed her by the wrist and jerked her forward, making her stumble into him. Then, he sat down on his chair, and began to pull her across his lap.

"What the hell are you doing?"

"I mentioned consequences, did I not?"

"Put me down!"

"Momentarily." He put a hand in the small of her back to keep her still, and began lifting the hem of her dress up her sleek, nyloned legs. He was a little surprised to see the stockings she wore, thigh high and clipped to a garter belt. It left the tops of her thighs bare up to the rising crescent moons of her butt.

"Stop! Put me down!"

"I will, Elizabeth. As soon as you've been punished."

"No!"

There could be no doubt now that he was about to spank her for her insolence. She began to kick up her heels, and Mr. Shern trapped her legs with one of his own. She was stuck now, face down across his lap, and still his hand rose up her legs, taking her dress with it.

Now the material of her dress was scrunched around her waist, and Mr. Shern got his first view of her compact, nicely rounded bottom. Pert domes rose underneath royal blue panties, clinging to her ass like a second skin.

He decided: now would not be the right time to lower those panties and reveal her cute womanly bottom for a good, solid spanking. It was too soon; and there would ample opportunity later, he was sure. But for now, he pulled the material up her cheeks a bit, letting more skin spill out the sides, and giving her a thick wedgie. Perversely, he pulled the top hem of the panties up her back, letting her get a feel of the tight material stuffed up her crack. Elizabeth grunted and yelled some more.

"Stop it!"

SMACK!

He slapped her ass, hard, right across her cheeks, and Elizabeth shrieked.

"Stop!"

SMACK!

"STOP IT!"

SMACK!

"Let me up right now--"

SMACK SMACK SMACK SMACK--

"You son of a bitch--"

SMACK!

"Bastard!"

SMACK!

She kept hollering, and he kept smacking. She twisted, she writhed, she kicked; but Mr. Shern kept up his steady drumming, keeping her trapped across his lap, slapping her ass with a stinging palm. After a few moments, she began to scream.

"Please, stop, please!"

He paused his hand midair. "Ah, now you are asking, not ordering. Better. But you forgot to say 'Sir.' Say 'please stop, Sir,' and promise to be honest in your answers, and I'll stop." He gave her another second, but when she didn't answer right away, he started spanking her again; only now his hand rose and fell harder and faster, not giving her any break between smacks. Mr. Shern watched as her cheeks wobbled and cringed under his steady assault. She had very sensitive skin. It was already a blushing red.

"Okay, okay! Please stop, Sir! Please stop, Sir!"

"And you'll be honest from now on?"

"Yes!"

"Yes, what?"

"Yes, Sir!" Her voice cracked before it broke.

Mr. Shern immediately stopped, lifted her off his lap, and let her dress fell back into place.

"There now, see how fast it stops when you listen?"

She rubbed her butt across her dress and looked at him murderously, like an angry child after a hard spanking.

"Keep that in mind," he said. "Remember it for next time."

"There won't be a next time. I'm going home!"

"Oh? You're giving up? Running away with your tail between your legs? Very well. I will summon the liaison to take you back to your room. I'm surprised, though, Elizabeth. I thought you were stronger than this." He challenged her with his words, and by the expressions running across her face, knew exactly what she was thinking.

He hadn't mentioned her father; he didn't see the need. But he did, in fact, know full well that she would have to face some pretty steep consequences back home if she didn't stay the full three days and do everything he ordered. Loss of her passport. More restrictions. Less allowance. And those were the easy ones. She had to weigh her choices: deal with Mr. Shern for three days, or deal with her father and stepmother for God only knew how long.

But the way he had worded it, twisted it into a scornful dismissal, was what really got to her. He had insinuated she wasn't strong enough--she wasn't even worth his effort. Well, she would show him how willful she could be.

"I'll stay," she said.

He smiled. "Then sit," he gestured her back into the chair. Elizabeth sat down gingerly, shifting her gait a bit as she did. Mr. Shern pretended not to notice.

"So. When you fucked these boys--did you ever orgasm?"

Elizabeth lowered her head in shame. "No," she murmured.

Mr. Shern paused. "Have you ever experienced an orgasm by yourself? By playing with your clit?"

Now Elizabeth's face was bright red. "Yes," she whispered. "I have."

"How did you make yourself come? With an open hand? Your fingers? A sex toy?"

"My--my fingers."

"Which fingers?"

The questioning went on and on, Mr. Shern demanding to know how she touched herself, how she had touched the boys she had slept with, how they had touched her; what positions she had tried, with the boys, by herself. He even wanted to know if she'd fucked in the dark, or with the lights on.

At last, the questions tapered off, and Mr. Shern seemed satisfied. "I think I have a good idea where we need to begin," he said. "So let's get started."

"Started? Started with what?"

"Why, your sex training, Elizabeth. It is why you are here." Elizabeth gaped at him, and Mr. Shern frowned. "Did your stepmother not tell you?"

"She told me I might appreciate learning a few, um, *things*....she said the staff at the Hotel Bentmoore would be able to show me a good time...."

"Yes, all that is true."

"But she never called it *sex training,*" Elizabeth said, feeling tricked. She would have a few choice words for her stepmother when she got home.

"Well, if you object to the term, we won't use it. Think of it exactly like your stepmother said: I can show you a good time--if you are good, and obey." He grinned wolfishly, and for the first time, she looked scared. "Now don't worry, I'm here to help you. We'll do this together." He put his hand out. "Come here."

"Here, where?"

"Here, to me," he crooked his finger at her, and Elizabeth took the two steps needed to come up to his chest. She could feel the heat radiating off him, the male allure. He was slightly tan, muscled in the all the right places, and stood proudly before her in a very confident, dominant way. She got a good whiff of his male scent, and closed her eyes; she would *not* allow herself to become attracted to this man, especially not after the way he had spanked her.

But it was too late. He overpowered her senses just by standing there, and the need rose within her, clearing her head of everything else, making her aware of nothing but him. When she opened her eyes, it was to stop herself from literally swaying into him. Mr. Shern smiled down at her, recognizing her reaction.

"You don't have to hide your attraction to me, Elizabeth. I find you very attractive, too. But unlike you, I know how to handle my sexual desire. So: lesson number one. Touch me."

The words thrilled her and shocked her at the same time. She had a feeling she would be going through a lot of shocks and surprises in this room for the next few days.

"Touch you, how?"

"Any way you want. Explore, get creative. Let your fingers guide you, I'm sure you'll get the hang of it. I won't stop you."

With slow, gentle hands, Elizabeth pressed her fingers to Mr. Shern's arms. The skin was smooth and warm, but she could feel the hard muscle underneath. She trailed her fingers up his shoulders, down his chest, letting them skim across his stomach and abs. Mr. Shern had no chest hair, and his nipples were small and brown, flat against his pectorals.

Feeling bold now, Elizabeth circled him from behind, and let her fingers trail his sloping back, running her knuckles down his spine. He arched, goosed a bit, and she smiled. She went back to facing him, ready to resume her slow exploration, but he grabbed her hand.

"Your turn."

"You want to touch me?"

"No. I want you to touch yourself." Her eyes widened in alarm. "It's nothing you haven't done before, right?" He asked her. "You just have an audience this time. Do whatever you would normally do to yourself."

She opened her mouth as if to object, then shut it and stepped away from him, looking unsure. But with slow movements, she reached behind her back and began to unzip her dress, pulling it off her arms.

"Put it on the chair," Mr. Shern ordered, his mouth dry. Elizabeth, undressed down to her underwear and stockings, was a sight to behold. With a high, narrow waist and flaring hips, she looked like a school boy's dream. But he was no school boy, and he would be patient.

Elizabeth cupped her breasts, pushing them up inside her bra.

"No," Mr. Shern said. "Not through the bra. Take it off."

"But--"

"Now," he growled.

After giving it a moment of thought, Elizabeth complied. He was not saying *he* was going to touch her; he was saying she should touch herself. That made all the difference, in her opinion: she could touch herself however she wanted to, and he would just watch. And really, if she were as worldly as she claimed to be, this should be nothing for her.

But still, her fingers shook as she unclasped her bra and flung it on the chair. She had never simply undressed in front of a man before. Her breasts wobbled a bit as she moved: they were, indeed, perfectly pare shaped, with upstanding dusky nipples.

She ran her fingers over her breasts, cupping them lightly, then tweaked each nipple. She closed her eyes.

"No," Mr. Shern said quickly. "Keep your eyes open. On me."

Elizabeth held his stare, frozen for a moment. Then, she resumed her slow exploration of her breasts, her face slightly pink but steadfast. He looked into her eyes as she touched her breasts, never wavering, and she met the challenge head on, locking him in a staring contest of wills.

But after a few minutes, it was obvious all the nipple stimulation was getting to her. Her breath became heavy and uneven, and her eyes clouded in sexual heat.

"That's enough," Mr. Shern said. "My turn again. Come here and touch me."

Easily this time, Elizabeth walked up and began to trail his chest.

"No," Mr. Shern stopped her. "Lower this time. Take off my pants."

Elizabeth swallowed hard. Another new experience: she had never undressed a man before. But this was something she was actually excited to do, and she lowered to her knees quickly, undoing his pants and yanking them down. Mr. Shern was a bit surprised by her happy compliance, but didn't show it.

His cock sprang free, swollen and semi-erect, and Elizabeth got her first up close and personal look at the male anatomy. She took in his shape, the width and length of his cock, the way the veins ran under the skin and the top mushroomed to a bulbous head. She watched, mesmerized, as his ball sack contracted and relaxed, shifting under the gentle weight inside, the skin undulating hypnotically. Like his chest, Mr. Shern's balls were hairless and smooth.

"Go ahead, touch them." The man could read her thoughts. Elizabeth raised her hand and carefully cupped his balls, testing their weight. Mr. Shern kicked his pants across the floor and spread his feet.

Without realizing she was even doing it, Elizabeth had brought her face down all the way to her host's balls. He could feel her warm breath against the base of his cock, and it rose as it hardened. Elizabeth watched the process in fascination: she had never seen anything like it.

Then, without a bit of hesitation, she circled her fist around his dick and began to move it up and down.

"None of that yet," Mr. Shern said quickly, stopping her hand. "It's your turn again." He raised her up and pointed across the room. "Go to the bed."

Like a good girl, Elizabeth crawled across the bed, taking a seat right in the middle.

"Lie down, take off your panties."

"Uh--"

"I'm not going to touch you. I'm only going to watch you--but you're going to keep your eyes on me. Don't look away as you touch yourself. Let me see the pleasure in your eyes."

Her eyes furrowed, and she swallowed; but she lay back, hooked her fingers into the hem of her panties, and pulled them off her body. She was completely naked now, revealed and vulnerable, and did her best to fight the urge to cover herself with her hands.

Mr. Shern kept her gaze. But even keeping his eyes focused on hers, he could still see the apex of her thighs, the somewhat thick bulging mound of her pussy, the vaginal lips that were closed together as if locked in a kiss. A strip of light strawberry blond hair divided her pussy mound right down the middle, but otherwise, Elizabeth was shaved bare.

She brought her hand to her pelvis and rested it there, building up her nerve. Then, with slow determination, she glided it between her pussy lips, right into her soft, pink cunt.

"Very good," Mr. Shern said. "Take your time. We're in no rush."

Elizabeth moved her hand up and down, just a little bit, and was surprised by the thrilling electric shocks she felt. She was turned on, alright: her pussy felt swollen and warm, and tingled from the touch of her fingers. But it was embarrassing to be reacting this way in front of Mr. Shern, who looked completely in control of himself as she gasped and jerked. She closed her eyes.

"Eyes open!" Mr. Shern yelled. Elizabeth's eyes sprang open. "Keep them on me," Mr. Shern reminded her. "Keep going."

Elizabeth could feel her face going red as she did what he ordered; she felt like she was blushing all over her body. It was humiliating to be playing with herself in front of this man, shameful, embarrassing....but it was exciting, too. It had become very obvious by Mr. Shern's upstanding cock that he liked what he saw; he enjoyed the show she was giving him. It filled Elizabeth with a raw sense of female power she had never felt before.

Emboldened, Elizabeth opened her legs and pulled apart her pussy lips, opening herself up completely and letting her host get a good look at her delicate folds inside, the pearly pink labia and soft protective clitoral hood. With two fingers, she began to glide her hand across her cunt.

She tried to act cavalier and coy. She tried to control her expressions, looking at him neutrally as he gazed at her. But the erotic thrill of touching herself in front of such a strong, dominating male figure, who was also watching her every move and expression, was too much for her, and she couldn't control the twitches that quivered across her body or the heaving rise and fall of her breasts.

But she could control her hand. She would *not* let herself become so excited that she climaxed in front of this man. She would not let him see her jerking across the bed, completely oblivious in her own ecstasy, while he stood impassively by and watched.

So she purposefully moved her hand in slow, gentle circles, never increasing the tempo, never pushing herself too far. She was excited, obviously fully aroused-- but she would not make herself come.

Mr. Shern knew what she was up to, and had a way to deal with that.

He walked over to the wardrobe and came back carrying what looked like a large, purple dick.

"Do you know what this is?"

"Yes," she said nervously. "It's a vibrator." But she'd never held one before--she'd only seen them in pictures and on television.

"That's right." He turned the knob at the base, and the vibrator began to hum in his hand. "Take it, put it in your pussy."

"But--"

"No buts--unless it's me spanking yours again?"

With a scowl, Elizabeth grabbed the wicked vibrator out of his hand and lay back down. She took a minute to look at it: it was shiny, wide and smooth like a real cock, and hummed madly in her hand. Gingerly, she lowered it between her legs.

"Oh!"

The shock of the vibrations hit her swollen, nerve-filled pussy immediately, and Elizabeth closed her legs in automatic reaction, tensing up her muscles and lifting slightly off the bed with her feet. But she had closed her eyes again.

"Eyes on me, Elizabeth!" Mr. Shern thundered. She opened her eyes and looked at him. Hers were full of alarm now, as she began to get the full effect of the vibrating toy working against her.

She tried not to hold it too close to her clit, so that the silicone shell just barely touched her skin. But that didn't work; she could still feel it. In fact, it seemed to make her problem worse, as the delicious tickle of the vibrations only filled her with a greater need. Her pelvic muscles tensed up in response, and her clit began to throb.

She pressed the vibrator in, pushing it against the focal point of her pleasure nerves, and gasped. She could feel the wild vibrations all the way to her toes...it was heaven, sheer delight, like nothing she had ever felt before. She closed her eyes.

"Eyes open! Look at me!"

Again she opened them to stare at Mr. Shern obstinately. But soon, her eyes clouded with arousal, and Elizabeth couldn't hide the needy, almost pained expressions that flitted across her face.

Do not come, do not come, do not come while he stands there watching you....

But she was fighting a losing battle. Mr. Shern would keep her there, force her to stimulate herself with the vibrator and look him in the eyes at the same time, until she came. He was patient; he could wait. Like he'd said, they were in no rush. But it *would* happen. The only person keeping her from going over the edge was Elizabeth herself.

Elizabeth lasted as long as she could. Sweat began to bead down her face and sides, and her breathing came out in short, ragged gasps. She twisted, she arched, she opened and closed her legs; but she could not control her deep sexual need, the ache in her pelvis spreading inside her body. The blood rushed inside her, hot and fast, pounding in her ears like drums. She knew, instinctively, that the longer she waited, the more intense her final climax would be, and she would not be able to control her reactions at all.

But still, she held on. And all the while, Mr. Shern's eyes never let hers go; he was trying to break her, Elizabeth was sure...bend her to his will and use his devil's eyes to bore into her soul.

At last, she could take no more, and despite her final, vein attempt to hold back, the orgasm exploded from her throbbing pussy and pulsated across her entire body.

"OHH--" She pressed the humming toy against her clit hard, scissoring her legs and arching her back off the bed. This time, Mr. Shern let her close her eyes; she had lost all control over her actions anyway. But he noted the way her face flushed red, how the lines across her forehead deepened in overwhelming ecstasy as she came.

The waves of orgasm washed over her, and then her face relaxed completely as the waves receded, making her shiver now and then from the tiny ripples still rocking her limber body.

When she was done, she lifted the vibrator away from her clit, still humming away, and lay sprawled on the bed. Then, she opened her eyes and looked at her host tenaciously, the aftereffects of her powerful orgasm still making her tremble.

"You've done very well," Mr. Shern said. He grabbed the toy from her hand, turned it off, and went to the wardrobe. When he came back, he was belting a robe around himself. "You may relax for a few moments before getting dressed."

Elizabeth raised herself on the bed. "What happens now?" She asked.

"For now, you're done. The liaison will return you to me tomorrow morning."

"But what about...you?"

"Me? You don't have to worry about me. It's nice of you to ask, though," he said, grinning. Elizabeth pursed her lips.

"What happens tomorrow morning?"

"We will continue with your training."

Elizabeth hugged her knees to her chest. She decided she didn't really want to know yet what *that* would mean.

Everything felt different now. Mr. Shern had seen her come-face; he'd watched her...no, he'd *studied* her as she orgasmed, taking note how she reacted and how long it took for her to lose all control and any shred of resistance. Her orgasm had been like nothing she'd ever felt before...but was it worth the loss of her dignity?

Did she really have any choice?

"Time to get up," Mr. Shern interrupted her thoughts, smiling as if, once more, he knew exactly what she was thinking. "Eat well. I'll see you in the morning."

"And if I don't come?"

"Oh, believe me, you'll come."

"That's not what I meant," she said softly, embarrassed. She zipped up her dress and wiggled her feet into her shoes, brushing her fingers through her tossled hair. Mr. Shern pressed the button for the liaison.

"I know. Suffice it to say, you will come back. You will come when you are summoned or you will come later, but eventually, Elizabeth, you will have to return to this room and deal with me. The question is, do you want to see what happens if you test my patience?" He made his words sound casual, but the veiled threat was there.

She looked down. "No, Sir," she said.

"Good girl," he replied. "I'll see you tomorrow." The liaison arrived and escorted her out of the room.

*****

The next day, when Elizabeth entered Mr. Shern's activity room, she looked like a much different girl from the one who had been there the day before. She wore a simple t-shirt and loose sweatpants, clean but worn. Slip on sneakers covered her feet. She had done nothing with her hair other than brush it, though it looked lovely all the same. She looked like a typical lazy teenager, waking up late on a Saturday morning.

Mr. Shern did not approve.

"You should always take some care with your appearance, Elizabeth," he told her sternly. "No matter where you are, or whom you're with, you should take some interest in how you look."

"But why?" She asked haughtily. "I am here to be trained in sex. Sex involves nakedness. Look at you-- you're only a wearing a robe. I'll be getting undressed anyway, so what does it matter what I'm wearing when I walk in?"

"Because it shows people how you think about yourself. It's a reflection on *you*," he tried to explain to her. "You are lovely, and you should show off that loveliness, not hide it behind drab clothes and an arrogant attitude. Don't you want people to see how beautiful you are? Or you don't want them to care?"

"Of course I want people to care," she shot back.

"Then show them you care about *yourself*," he said. "Dress to make yourself feel beautiful, and other people will notice."

Elizabeth looked down in thought. Her stepmother had tried many times to tell her exactly what Mr. Shern was telling her right now, but somehow, coming from him, it sounded different. She would take the advice to heart--although she would never admit it to *him*.

"You're right about one thing, though," he continued. "You are here for sex training, and that means getting naked. Since we've already seen each other's bodies, and very intimately, too, I see no reason to be bashful now. Take off your clothes." He held her stare, locking her eyes to his.

Without looking away, Elizabeth took off her clothes and laid the garments on a nearby chair.

"Good," he said, nodding his head and disrobing himself. His cock was slightly thickened, but not hard; it hung stiffly down, as if trying to decide which way to go.

She expected him to beckon her towards him, as he had the day before; but instead, he took her hand and led her to the bed, urging her onto it before he climbed in after her.

"Today, we are going to start with what you are already used to," he said. He dipped his head down to her nipples and began to suck.

Mr. Shern was no amateur, he knew how to treat a pair of female breasts to bring the owner to immediate and intense sexual arousal, and Elizabeth was now his victim. She had never felt anything like it, and quivered as his tongue flicked and poked her sensitive peaks. He sucked them deeper into his mouth, pulling and squeezing them with his lips. She dug her fingers into his hair, trying to keep his face still, but he moved from one upstanding nipple to the other, making them glisten and swell.

His hands began to roam over her body, her ribs, her hips, her stomach...Elizabeth began to gasp and moan, and she tilted back, giving herself up to his expert lips and hands. For a long time, he simply worked her over, getting her to a state of mindless need, until she was nothing but a bundle of raw nerves, waiting for soothing release.

He pushed her down on her back, spread her legs, and poked between her pussy lips with his warm, thick tongue.

"Oh God!" Elizabeth cried out from the erotic thrill of feeling his hot tongue poking past her outer gate, circling over her clitoral hood. With knowing hands, he spread her pussy lips, getting a good look at her hidden folds, and widened his tongue for a long, gentle lick.

Elizabeth squirmed and wiggled in sexual heat, but with steady hands, Mr. Shern kept her thighs still, and licked her until he had the helpless woman writhing in abandon.

But when she was about to come, he stopped.

"What? What just happened?" She asked, confused. He looked up at her from between her legs, and Elizabeth thought she had never seen anything so erotic in her life.

"You are not to come this way," he said. "Are you about to come?"

"I was," she admitted.

"Don't," he said. "If you feel like you are about to come, tell me. Understand?"

"I...I guess," she said. He dipped his head down and began to lick her once more, and Elizabeth dug her fingers into the sheets.

After a few moments, she could feel her pelvis tightening in a familiar way, and groaned.

"I'm...I'm..."

Mr. Shern stopped and lifted his head. Elizabeth took some ragged breaths, making some throaty cries with each one.

"Why are you doing this to me?"

"Because I don't want you to come this way. I only want you to *want* to come." He lowered his head and began to lap at her folds; but this time he took her clit and hood in his mouth and began to gently pull them with his soft lips. Her head swam and her muscles clenched; she arched from the sheets.

"Oh...oh..."

He stopped. Fury filled her.

"What the hell are you trying to do to me? This is driving me crazy!"

"I know," he said. "You need to learn control. You need to let the feeling build inside, learn how to hold it back, and when to release. You need to recognize how it feels right *before* you go over the edge, so you can keep yourself going longer."

"But I can't!" She wailed. She tried to pull away from him, and he pushed her legs back down. She tried to get up from the bed, and he clamped her hands down with his. She looked at him, defiantly, breathing hard; things had moved beyond a simple argument, now, and they both knew it. She was fighting his will.

"Stay here," he said, and padded to the wardrobe. Elizabeth watched him go in confusion, then furrowed her brows when she saw what he held in his hands as he returned.

"What are those?" She asked suspiciously.

"Tools to help you to obey," he said. He climbed over her and grabbed one of her wrists, flinging metal over it, and Elizabeth heard it click and lock. He grabbed her other wrist, locking metal around that one, too; and before she knew it, her hands were cuffed together.

"Hey!"

Paying her no heed, he straightened her arms up above her head, grabbed the foot long chain connecting the two cuffs, and looped it into the hook concealed behind the mattress. Elizabeth was now chained to the wall.

But Mr. Shern wasn't done. Rebuffing her struggles, he cuffed her ankles, too, and chained each one to a corner of the bed, so that she was spread wide, and completely vulnerable.

This time, when he spread open her pussy lips and extended his tongue, Elizabeth tried to squirm away. But it was useless; in fact, her squirming just made her predicament worse. He kept his tongue still, letting it glide over her wet slit, as she gyrated her body. When she was still, he moved, lapping her soft layers like a cat eating cream.

But every time she was on the verge of coming, Mr. Shern would stop and wait for her to calm down. Her frustration was driving her crazy, and she struggled against the cuffs, but Mr. Shern would not let her come.

This was worse than yesterday, she decided. At least then, she felt like she had a measure of control; now she had none.

When Mr. Shern lifted his head again, effectively cutting her off from another orgasm, Elizabeth cried out in fury and need. With no sense of dignity left, she did the only thing that had worked on him before: she begged.

"Please! Please let me come! Sir, Please!"

Mr. Shern looked at her shrewdly. He knew she was as close to the edge as he could get her; any touch now to her clitoris, the barest rub, and she'd likely explode. But that wasn't the way he wanted her to go.

He unlocked her ankles and Elizabeth closed her legs, grimacing from sexual arousal so great, it felt very close to pain. He unlooped the chain trapping her hands over her head from the hook in the wall, but pulled it with him as he lay down on his back, so that Elizabeth was forced to straddle his stomach, catching herself as she fell onto his chest.

"What are you doing?" She demanded. Not all the starch had gone out of her, it seemed.

"You're going to come with a man inside you," he said. "Ride me."

She sat up straight across his midsection, feeling his hard cock touching her ass.

"But how--"

"Put me inside you."

She twisted her arms around, but the chain between her cuffs wouldn't let her get both hands behind her back to maneuver him inside.

"And how am I supposed to do that?"

"With your hips," he said. With his hands on her shoulders, he grinded her down across his pelvis until her cunt was at the base of his cock. "Lift up and fit me in."

She lifted and shifted, feeling the head of his cock against her pussy; and when she got it right at the entrance to her cunt, she slid down. It went in slick and hard, filling her up until she was stuffed with stiff, thick cock. She felt impaled.

"Sit up a little," Mr. Shern said gruffly. Elizabeth complied, feeling him even deeper inside her. She gasped. "Now move," he ordered.

Elizabeth moved. She glided him up and down; she grinded her hips against his; she undulated above him, so that her cunt muscles contracted tight, gripping his cock in a warm, wet vise. But after a few minutes, she found a rhythm she liked, and began to rock back and forth, letting him glide a bit in and out as he churned against her clit.

"Oh. Oh. Oh--"

Her cries became louder and more desperate as she rocked back and forth against his prick, unable to control herself.

"Oh OH--"

Mr. Shern reached up and pinched her nipples between his fingers, flicking them with his fingertips. Meanwhile, Elizabeth bucked wildly, making the bed groan and shake.

It didn't take long for her to climax; and when she did, she arched her back in a perfect curve, thrusting her hips over his groin in mad fury and crying out in ecstasy. Her cunt muscles squeezed him deliciously, spasming all around his thick length, and Mr. Shern came, too, shooting his cum right up her squeezing cunt. She fell on top of his chest, breathing hard.

After a moment, when he felt his deflated cock shrinking from her cunt grip, Mr. Shern lifted her over to his side and unlocked her cuffs.

"Rest for how long you need," he said gently. He went to the chair and grabbed his robe. "You may have the rest of the day to yourself. I will have the liaison bring you back after dinner....let's say, seven o'clock? Until then, you may enjoy the hotel."

Elizabeth could only nod; she was still breathing hard. She flopped across the bed, stretched her relaxed muscles, and rose to retrieve her clothes. She felt very good--not just from the incredible orgasm, but from a sense of fulfillment. She had come with a man inside her, from grinding against his rock hard prick. It was like she had popped her cherry all over again, but in a much better way.

"Just one thing, Elizabeth," Mr. Shern said. "Don't wander away from the hotel. Stay inside, or go relax by one of the pools--but no touring. We have enough to do here at the hotel that you shouldn't get bored by dinnertime. Understand?"

"Yes, Sir," she answered. She really wasn't bothered by the order. She had been planning on relaxing around the pool anyway.

"Good," he said, and pressed the button to summon the liaison. "I'll see you after dinner, then."

*****

After showering and eating, Elizabeth felt invigorated, and decided to ask at the front desk what kind of amenities the hotel had to offer. She knew they had tennis and horseback riding, but didn't feel like doing anything that would involve changing into different clothes.

"We have yoga and dance classes...but you would have to change for those, too," the woman behind the counter said. Tall and elegantly dressed, the woman put a finger to her chin and looked away in thought. "We have hiking guides. They meet down by the stables, and leave every half hour. The guides follow the trails around the hotel." She took out a map and traced with her finger some of the different routes the hiking guides took.

"A short hike sounds nice," Elizabeth said, looking at the map.

"A group is leaving in ten minutes," the woman told her. "Do you know where the stables are?"

"I'll find it," Elizabeth replied.

But finding the stables, as loud and odorous as they were, took longer than Elizabeth thought it would, and by the time she found the guides' departure point, the group she had meant to join had already left. Instead of waiting for the next one, Elizabeth decided to follow the trail down herself and meet up with the guide further on.

It was a mistake. Elizabeth followed the wrong trail, and didn't realize it until she had walked for a good thirty minutes. Remembering the map, she brashly thought she could figure out a short cut to the right trail. But when she couldn't find it, she decided to go back to the first trail she'd been following, and retrace her steps to the hotel. Another mistake.

Very soon she realized none of the rocky scenery looked familiar anymore. She was completely lost.

She didn't panic at first. She couldn't have gone far from the hotel; a few miles at most. People hiked the area all the time, and there was bound to be a landmark somewhere. Eventually, she would find help.

But when two hours went by and Elizabeth hadn't seen or heard a single soul, fear began to creep into her. She had not worn good hiking shoes, she had thought she'd just be taking a short stroll around the area, and now her feet were killing her. The sun was bright and hot against her skin. She had no hat and no water.

When she came to a mountain of rocks, Elizabeth decided to climb to the top and get a better view of her surroundings. This was yet another mistake: when she got to the top, she fell, sliding all the way down the hill until she came to a dusty stop on her side. She sat up and took stock of herself: her calf was scratched and bleeding, and her shirt was ripped. But she was basically okay, nothing was sprained or broken. And the small glimpse she'd managed at the top of the hill had afforded her one thing: a view of a road, right beyond the rocks.

Her luck changed when a car drove past quickly, just as she began to follow the road in the direction of the hotel...she hoped.

"You okay, miss?" The man at the wheel lowered his window just enough to take in her sweaty, dusty appearance. His expression was one of open concern. He looked boyish and innocent, not threatening in the least. Some cool air from the air conditioning inside his car wafted out the open window, caressing Elizabeth's hot cheeks.

"I kind of need a ride," she said. "Do you know the Hotel Bentmoore?"

"Yeah, it's a few miles down. You need a ride there?"

"Please," Elizabeth answered, and ran around to the passenger door. She got in gratefully, relaxing against the seat as he drove.

"You a guest at the hotel?" Her savior asked skeptically, glancing at her as he watched the road.

"Yeah, I'm staying there for a couple days."

"So how did you end up out here, alone?"

"I wanted to take a hike, but the group left without me, and then I got lost...." she looked at her calf, smeared with dried blood.

"Oh wow, you cut yourself up good. You sure you're okay?"

"I'll be okay," she said, grimacing as she took stock of the long, deep scratches. She had been lucky, she supposed: she could have been hurt a lot worse. She could have cut up her face.

"If Mr. Shern finds out...." she murmured.

"What was that?"

"Nothing." She could see the view of the hotel coming up ahead of them. She thought her driver would pull up to the front entrance and drop her off; but instead, he parked near a side door, and got out himself.

"Come," he said, holding the door open for her. "Let's get you bandaged up." He opened a locked side door of the hotel with a key he had on a ring.

"You work here?" Elizabeth asked in surprise.

"Yup," he said. But he offered her no more information as he led her down a tiled corridor, lined on each side with closed doors. Elizabeth had no idea where they were inside the hotel. Then her companion motioned her into a door that had a sign on it, "First Aid."

"Stay here. I'll get someone to help you with your leg." He disappeared, and Elizabeth sat down on the narrow cot by the wall. After a moment, she went into the adjoining bathroom, and used the toilet, sink and mirror to freshen herself up as best she could. The rest would have to wait until she got to her room.

A woman soon arrived, carrying a first aid kit and a tall glass of water, and got to work cleaning and dressing Elizabeth's leg, as Elizabeth drank gratefully. The alcohol stung like hell, and the scratches bled anew. But they were clean now, and wouldn't get infected; and the water managed to perk her up.

As soon as Elizabeth walked out of the First Aid room, ready to go up to her room and take a relaxing bath, she saw her liaison. The man must have been waiting for her outside for quite a while, she realized.

"Mr. Shern would like to see you downstairs immediately," her liaison informed her blandly.

"Right now?" Elizabeth looked down at herself, wondering how she could possibly hide what had happened to her, and then realized it was probably too late. Somehow, Mr. Shern already knew: that was why he wanted to see her. But how had he learned so quickly?

"Okay," she sighed, mentally preparing herself for the confrontation. She followed the stoic back of her liaison all the way downstairs, hugging her elbows to her chest as the elevator descended. Mr. Shern would be angry. Probably very angry. Would he scream at her? Maybe even spank her again?

She stopped at her usual activity room door, but her liaison walked on.

"Mr. Shern is in a different room," he turned to say. "This way, please."

The room he let her into was darker than her usual one, and full of strange pieces of furniture that Elizabeth couldn't identify or begin to understand. But she didn't take very much notice of the design of the room: her eyes were on the two men standing in front of her. One was her host, Mr. Shern...and the other was her savior, the man who had driven her to the hotel.

"What are you doing here?" she asked him now, realizing that somehow, she'd been played.

"I told you, I work here," he said. He looked at Mr. Shern, but Mr. Shern did not look back; his focus was all on Elizabeth.

"I tell you not to leave the hotel, a simple enough request...and find out a mere few hours later that you have completely disobeyed me," he said, his eyes full of cold fury.

"It wasn't my fault," Elizabeth began. "I just wanted to go for a hike, I thought I could find the trail--"

"You didn't think at all," Mr. Shern shouted at her, revealing his full blown anger for the first time. "This hotel is in the middle of the desert. Mr. Sinclaire tells me you had no sun protection, no hat--and you were lost. You had no fucking *guide*, and no idea where the hell you were going."

157

"Look, I've paid the price," she said, showing him her bandaged leg. "I won't do it again."

"So you got a little cut up. Elizabeth, you could have *broken* your leg, do you understand that? You could have broken your *neck*. You could have died out there, and no one would have known it."

"I get it, I get it. I'm sorry." She cast her eyes down demurely. Then, looking up at him with half hooded eyes, she pouted her lips out *just* a bit and raised her eyebrows, giving him her full, charmingly innocent look. This look had worked on two headmasters and countless of teachers, not to mention many boys, to keep her out of trouble. Elizabeth had learned over the years that once she turned on the charm, no hot blooded man could resist her.

Except, apparently, Mr. Shern. And the man standing next to him, as well, who simply sighed and rolled his eyes before looking sideways at his companion.

"Would you like some help?" He asked cryptically. "Everything is in the wardrobe; nothing is set out."

"I'll find what I need, thank you," Mr. Shern said quietly, never looking away from Elizabeth, who now felt the first prickling of true fear.

"Very well," the man named Mr. Sinclaire said. "I have the room booked in three hours. Will that be enough time?"

"Three hours will be plenty."

"I'll leave you to her, then."

He pressed the button for the liaison. Then, as if remembering something brilliant, he turned around once more.

"Shall I have some ginger sent down from the kitchen....?" Once again, Elizabeth had no idea why her host would want food of all things...but she didn't ask.

Mr. Shern took a long time to answer. The door opened, and the liaison held it steady; and still, Mr. Shern stared at Elizabeth, thinking.

"No," he finally decided. "I have what I need here. What you are suggesting would be too...premature."

The man shrugged. "Your decision," he said. "Good luck." He walked through the doorway, and Elizabeth heard it click in place behind him.

Mr. Shern regarded her silently, his expression unfathomable. Elizabeth swallowed hard, growing more nervous.

"I...I really am sorry," she said, trying to sound more sincere. "I didn't mean to get lost...it just kind of happened. I promise, from now on, I'll listen to you." She hoped her apology would appease him, at least a little, but Mr. Shern didn't respond. He didn't move in any way.

"What do you want from me?" She finally snapped. "It's not like I wanted to get my leg cut up. Say something, damn it!"

He sighed, and walked over to the wardrobe. The double doors of the upstanding closet opened; he rummaged around inside. And all the while, he said not a word.

When he closed the doors, he turned around, and Elizabeth got a first good look at what he was holding: cuffs and chains.

"No," she whispered. He strode towards her with purpose.

"You were warned; you disobeyed. You will be punished." His words were short and simple, but the way he took Elizabeth's wrist and calmly began to buckle it inside the cuff filled her growing dread.

He cuffed her other hand, too, before Elizabeth's fear finally snapped. But when the adrenaline finally hit her blood, unfreezing her feet, she ran across the room, trying to get to the other side of the bed.

Mr. Shern tackled her onto it. Elizabeth turned to face him, trying to fight him off; he hoisted her over his shoulder and carried her to the corner of the room. As he lowered her feet to the floor, he lifted her hands high above her head, and looped the chain between her cuffs into a hook set high into the ceiling.

Elizabeth was now stretched and chained to the ceiling. She rattled the chain, pulling on the hook; it would not move.

As Mr. Shern went back to the wardrobe to retrieve a few more things, Elizabeth hollered and struggled some more against the chain.

"Put me down right now! Put me down! Put--"

"Be quiet or I will gag you," he said. Elizabeth snapped her mouth shut. "You have no right to be upset, Elizabeth," he continued. "You did this to yourself. I gave you those orders for a reason. Did it even occur to you how reckless you were being? How close you were to being seriously hurt?"

"Nothing happened!" She yelled. "I got some cuts, that's all!"

"You spent hours in the hot sun, wandering around, lost. You got into the car of a complete stranger, trusting him not to hurt you."

"And how was I supposed to get out of the hot sun if I *didn't* get into the car?" She retorted. "The guy was nice! He even works here!"

"Do you always get into cars of men you don't know?" He asked. When she didn't answer, his eyes grew shrewd. "Don't you ever give *one thought* to your own safety? Your own actions?"

"I've been doing fine on my own till now," she snapped.

"Yes...till now," he said softly. "But this time...this time, my dear, you will pay the price for your careless-ness." He walked up to her, holding what looked like a ping-pong paddle.

Elizabeth closed her eyes and tried to calm herself. He had spanked her before, and she had lived. She would get through this, too. She would not let him see her fear.

He put the paddle under his arm as he closed the distance between them. "I gave you too much protection last time," he said. "I will not offer it again."

He yanked at her pants and panties, undressing her from the waist down in one fell swoop. Her clothes pooled at her feet and around her shoes.

"What the hell--"

"A proper spanking is done on a bare bottom," he said. Then, Mr. Shern circled her waist with one hand to keep her still, and raised the paddle up high in the air in the other.

WAP! WAP! WAP! WAP!

He paddled her pale, pliant cheeks with quick, sharp snaps of the wrist. Elizabeth arched herself forward reactively, but Mr. Shern held her in place, snapping at his twin targets with expert accuracy.

WAP--WAP--WAP--WAP--

He paddled her bottom faster now, alternating between her butt cheeks, watching them cringe together as he walloped her ass, the way they rippled after each smack. After a while, her butt began to blush crimson, and he noted how the blush spread across her tender cheeks, getting darker with each stroke of the paddle.

But all the while, Elizabeth kept herself from crying out. She clenched her teeth together, letting only a shallow hissing sound escape through her lips as the blows fell.

WAP--WAP--WAP--WAP--

Finally she couldn't keep quiet anymore, and let out a single, short shriek. She let out another after each snap of his wrist, letting her host know how badly the pain was flaring across her ass.

But Mr. Shern didn't alter his rhythm one bit. In fact, he seemed to speed up even more, adding a sharper flick with each *thwak* of the paddle.

After a few more moments, he stopped, and Elizabeth thought he was done. She breathed hard in relief, proud of herself for not embarrassing herself too badly.

Then Mr. Shern said nonchalantly, "I think that's enough of a warm up," and went back over to the wardrobe. This time, when he returned, he was carrying more cuffs, more chain, and what looked like a long, thin, rod.

He pulled Elizabeth's pants and undies away from her feet, taking her shoes with them. He cuffed her ankles, then spread them wide, chaining each one to another hook in the floor, so that they were about shoulder length apart. Elizabeth couldn't spin or twist like before; her feet were chained down in place. She couldn't even close her legs. Her pussy lips had opened slightly when he'd spread her wide, and they stayed open now, vulnerable to the open air.

"Do you know what this is, Elizabeth?" Mr. Shern now asked, coming around to face her. "It's a crop. Very thin, very flexible. Very painful." He bent it in tight and let it spring back with a hiss; it moved through the air in a blur.

"When you feel this, I want you to think about how much worse you could have been hurt out there. How awful it would have been to be in this much pain, alone, with no one to help you."

He stepped behind her and took aim.

WHIP!

Involuntarily, Elizabeth cried out. The pain was sharp indeed, like a tiny knife cutting across her skin.

WHIP! WHIP! WHIP! WHIP!

Each blow sliced into her bottom, already smarting from the paddling. But this was worse, so much worse than the paddle had been. She could hear the crop hiss through the air before it cut into her flesh, and she tensed up every muscle in her body to prepare for the inflaming sting. But there was no escape from the pain, no way to move away from it or make it stop.

I will not cry, I will not cry, I will not cry....The lines of pain began to criss-cross her sensitive flesh. There was no let up to the rhythm or force of the strokes, no time to recover between swipes of the crop; the string of hissing smacks blended one into the other, until the pain swelled into searing, white hot agony.

Elizabeth began to cry.

The whipping went on.

"Please!" She screamed. "Please stop! I can't, I can't...."

"You can't what? You can't handle the pain? What about handling *yourself* better from now on? Thinking before you do something? Taking control of your actions? Taking some responsibility?"

"I will, I will," she sobbed. "I promise I will."

"Not good enough, Elizabeth," he growled. "No more promises. Not this time." He whipped her ass again, and again, and again, and Elizabeth sobbed loudly now, all shred of her dignity gone. Each butt cheek burned like fire, and the crop continued to scald into her flesh new lines of humiliation.

"Say you'll take responsibility for your actions, Elizabeth. Say it."

"I'll...I'll take responsibility for my actions."

The crop came up between her legs this time, snapping against her inner thigh, biting into her sensitive flesh. Elizabeth gasped.

"I'll take responsibility for my actions!"

The crop came up again between her legs, biting into her other thigh.

"I'll take responsibility for my actions!"

The crop hissed through the air, flying up high between her spread legs, and landed with deadly accuracy right inside her pussy. Elizabeth screamed.

"I'll take responsibility for my actions! I'll take responsibility for my actions! I'll take--I'll take--" She couldn't go on; the sobs choked off her voice. She lowered her head in shame, crying freely and loudly like a child. She hadn't cried like this in years.

She didn't see Mr. Shern as he watched her, the outpouring of sympathy he offered in his expression...the concern in his eyes. Elizabeth's eyes were too flooded with tears to see.

For a brief second, Mr. Shern's face became tender, staring at her with something akin to longing...and then it hardened once more. She didn't need tenderness right now. She needed to *learn*. But she had taken as much as she could--it would be up to her to learn from this what she would.

He unchained her from the floor, working her ankles first, then unbuckling the wrist cuffs. As soon as her wrists were free, she crumpled against him, crying hard. And for a long time, he held her, rubbing her back and making soothing hushing noises. But within a few moments, she had collected herself enough to move away from him. She looked at him with weary eyes.

"Get dressed," he said abruptly, collecting her clothes and throwing them to her. She caught them reactively, but held them loosely in her hands. "Go back to your room, take a bath, have dinner. I will still meet with you later tonight. We will continue with your training as scheduled."

She went to the bed to sit down as she pulled on her pants, but stood up quickly when the burn hit her bottom. So she leaned against the bed instead, working as fast as she could before the liaison arrived.

He seemed to come in no time at all, but Elizabeth took slow steps towards the door. She was exhausted; her leg hurt; her ass was in agony. And she was supposed to return for more training? Tonight?

But the look Mr. Shern gave her as she walked out the door told her clearly: yes. She would return tonight to submit to his will, and obey his every command. She had no choice.

*****

The first thing Elizabeth did when she got to her room was go straight to the bathroom and turn on the water faucets in her jacuzzi tub. Then she closed the bathroom door as the water ran, and slowly pulled down her pants to get a good look at her smarting bottom behind the full length mirror.

Her whole butt was now an angry, flaming, striped red. It actually seemed to glow under her skin, a burning blush that covered her cheeks. Raised welts cut lines across her flesh, a shade lighter than the blush, like they had been branded into her. She poked at one of the darker welts with a careful finger, cringed in response, and cursed Mr. Shern under her breath.

As soon as there was enough water in the tub, she climbed in and turned the jets on. The hot water scalded her already burning ass even further, but she took her time, accustoming herself to the feel of the water against her skin. Soon, she was lying back languidly against the tub, resting her head on the small pillow the hotel had courteously provided.

She closed her eyes, felt her body relax, and let herself think.

She was angry at what Mr. Shern had done to her, the harsh beating her ass had endured by his hand. But she was surprised to realize that she wasn't really angry at *him*. In fact, what she felt for the man was a new measure of respect, and a small kernel of...gratitude. Maybe even the tiniest hint of appreciation.

No one had ever cared that much about what she did with herself, not her teachers, not her headmasters, and certainly not her father. They all had only been interested in her antics as far as making sure her wild behavior couldn't somehow be traced back to *them*. Beyond that, they didn't really care.

Mr. Shern had been the first man to ever be truly concerned for her own well-being, and demand from her some thought into her own behavior, her own future. Her host's lessons were hard, and they hurt...but they left her with new found understanding, too, and a better judgment of herself.

So when the liaison returned a few hours later to escort her once more to her host, Elizabeth was ready as expected.

She had pinned up her hair in a sweeping coif; her strawberry red highlights shined like strands of fire.

She wore a simple black chiffon dress and stiletto black shoes; both made her bare legs look long and shapely. But a large band-aid still adhered to her calf.

At this point, her leg was giving her much more pain than her bottom. In fact, after her relaxing bath and some ointment applied to the area, her ass hardly bothered her at all.

When she entered the activity room and heard the door shut behind her, she cast her eyes down and waited nervously. She was afraid Mr. Shern would make mention of her latest punishment, and any reference would only add to her humiliation.

But when she looked up, he was regarding her with a pleased expression, and Elizabeth understood that he would not bring up her whipping again. She had been punished, had paid the price for her actions, and now, it was time to move on.

"You look lovely," he said.

"Thank you," she answered, looking down again. Mr. Shern smiled, then decided it was time to get down to business.

"So far, we have been focusing on your own pleasure. How to control it, and how to be open to new experiences that will bring you to greater sexual arousal, so you can experience better, more intense orgasms. Tonight, you will begin to learn how to focus on the pleasure of your partner, and how doing so can intensify sexual fulfillment for the both of you."

Elizabeth listened avidly, wondering what he would have her do. Her answer came soon enough.

"Please take off your clothes."

She quickly moved to comply; but when she began to lower her side zipper, he stopped her.

"Not like that--you're not in any rush. Do it slowly, let me appreciate your curves. Look at me while you undress. I want to watch as you get turned on--and you should see how I get turned on."

She continued to unzip the rest of the dress, but slower this time, lowering it to her waist one sleeve at a time. She never looked away from his eyes as she moved, and could see in his how the little show she was putting on excited him. He had been right, she was getting turned on: her nipples poked out at him like hard pink nubbins, begging to be rubbed and flicked.

Without thinking about it, she wet two fingers and squeezed a nipple between them, twisting it a bit so that it protruded even more. She looked at him questioningly.

"Good, that's good," he said, his voice hoarse. "Now finish undressing."

She lowered the rest of her dress, stepping out of it one foot at a time, and flung it onto the nearest chair. Now she stood before him in nothing but a pair of thin nylon panties, sheer black, and her stiletto-heeled shoes. She shifted her legs a bit, moving her hips and making her breasts wobble, and Mr. Shern's throat went dry.

"Take off your shoes and come here," he said.

Slowly, she slipped out of her shoes and padded over to him. She moved in close, until her face was looking up at his and he could feel her warm breath against his chin. Her lips looked soft and wide, and her eyes gazed at him seductively. He would be getting a good feel of those lips tonight--but not against his mouth.

"Now undress me," he ordered. "You've already done this, you know what to do."

Immediately she complied, lowering herself down to her knees and unclasping his pants. As she pulled the clothes binding his legs down around his feet, his cock sprang free, tall and rigid. Now unencumbered from the constricting clothes, it seemed to grow even larger, and she watched in fascination.

Mr. Shern picked up his pants and threw them across the back of a chair. Then he looked down at Elizabeth expectantly.

"Your knowledge is sorely lacking when it comes to handling a man with your mouth," he said. "Thankfully, there are many ways to get this lesson right. I've found that the hardest obstacle facing most women is their simple fear and intimidation of the male phallus. But there is nothing to be afraid of, it will not hurt you--and as long as you treat it gently, give it some care, you will not hurt it, either. But I've also found that the best way to break a woman's hindering fear is through the use of her tongue. So: lick me."

Elizabeth looked up at him, confused. His cock was huge, and at this point, facing up proudly to the ceiling. *How* did he want her to lick him?

"Just get your tongue out and lick me however you want," he said, answering the question in her eyes. "Believe me, there are very few ways to get this wrong. Just get a taste for it for now."

Elizabeth dutifully stuck out her tongue and pressed it against his cock, getting her first real taste of male prick. It felt smooth, almost satiny against her tongue, but she could feel the bumps from the veins underneath the skin. Mr. shern inhaled sharply.

She widened her tongue now, and began to lick all the way up his cock, moving from base to tip, and had the satisfaction of hearing Mr. Shern gasp. For a while, she licked him like she would an ice cream cone, letting her tongue glide up his warm prick, then releasing it to start again at the base. But after a few moments, she realized there was really no reason to lift her tongue away, and began to glide it up and down in wide, even strokes.

"That's good," Mr. Shern said. "Now: do the balls. Gently...."

With her lips, she reached under his ballsack and carefully pressed her tongue against the soft tissue. She could feel Mr. Shern's twin eggs nestled inside, and was careful not to push against them too hard. But she licked the skin contracting all around, and when Mr. Shern widened his stance to give her better access, she licked his inner thighs, too. She licked until his entire scrotum was glistening with her saliva, burying her face between his legs and sticking her tongue all the way out to reach the under-arch of his balls. She breathed in his scent: Mr. Shern's balls had a unique smell to them, distinctly male, and she reacted instinctively, inhaling deeply.

"The head of the cock is the most sensitive spot," he said, continuing with the lesson. "Take it in your mouth, but be careful with your teeth."

Elizabeth straightened her back until her mouth leaned into the head of his prick, and then she pressed her lips to the soft tip, kissing it lovingly. Mr. Shern smiled down at her, appreciating her care; and then he closed his eyes, sinking into blissful delight, as she glided her mouth onto his dick. She kept a tight grip on him with her soft, heavenly lips.

Her mouth stayed tight around him, but between her lips, she flicked the tip of his cock with her tongue, jabbing at the nerve-filled hole, circling the bulbous head all around and tucking her tongue underneath the ridge; and Mr. Shern groaned in response, placing his hands on her shoulders to hold himself steady.

"Good, that is very good," he whispered. "Use your tongue...ah...yes...now suck me."

Elizabeth took the shaft in her mouth and sucked him like a bone.

"Ah, no...take me from the tip, like you did before, and suck your way down...yes, that's it...."

Elizabeth fixed her oral stance, lifting her head and taking the helmeted tip back in her mouth. But instead of gliding the shaft down, she sucked it into her mouth, pulling Mr. Shern's prick against her tongue. It tickled against the back of her throat, and she opened her jaws, swallowing him in, until her lips could almost touch his stomach.

"Yes, Elizabeth, that's it...yes..."

She sucked hard, making swallowing motions against his stiff prick with her tongue; and then she began to slide her warm delicious mouth up and down his glistening cock, sucking hard as she went, hollowing in her cheeks from the force of her pull.

Mr. Shern dug his hands into her hair, keeping her face from moving away from his swollen cock. As Elizabeth sucked him into her mouth, pulling him deeper down her throat, he began to thrust gently inside her, gliding his cock in and out, using her mouth like a warm, welcoming cunt. And Elizabeth thrust her mouth back, gobbling up his long prick like it was the most delicious thing in the world; and though she didn't know it, she was responding, too, bucking her hips and tightening the muscles in her cunt.

Her mouth moved quickly now as her head bobbed up and down against him. Her lips squeezed his hard cock, up and down, up and down...her tongue glided and flicked as he thrust inside her tight, hot mouth. She reached up and cupped his ball sack in her small, gentle hand, and Mr. Shern let out a throaty groan.

He arched his back and pumped into her face with total abandon, holding her steady by the back of her head. In the last second, Elizabeth could feel his prick go rock hard, straining against the soft confines of his skin; and then it exploded in her mouth.

Warm jets of Mr. Shern's cum shot down her throat as he pumped into her, completely lost in orgasmic delight. His cum tasted creamy and slightly salty, and Elizabeth swallowed it all, opening her jaws and gulping greedily as Mr. Shern's cock continued to erupt in her mouth. She sucked, and pulled, and swallowed some more; and when his thrusts began to subside and the cum only dribbled from his dick, she grabbed him by his backside and pushed him into her face, taking him down her throat for as long as she could.

At last, when he was completely done and Elizabeth had sucked his cock clean, he pulled out of her mouth and staggered to the bed.

"I give you this: you are a fast learner, Elizabeth," Mr. Shern said as he recovered his breath. Elizabeth grinned in pleasure. She remained on her knees, watching him recover, feeling very proud of herself. But she had not yet come herself, she had not been awarded that ultimate release, and now she was feeling very horny.

"Sir, are we...am I..." She didn't know how to continue with the question, or if she was even allowed to ask. But she was sorely afraid they were done for the night.

"Are we done? No, Elizabeth, we are not done," he said, looking stern. But Elizabeth sighed in relief, grinning in anticipation.

"So, next lesson. There are going to be times, like now, when your partner has climaxed before you. I know this has been a problem for you in the past, although it was for other reasons--your need to hold yourself back, among other things. But I don't think that's going to be an issue for you from now on." She didn't exactly nod in agreement, but cast her eyes down and gave him a tiny shrug.

"But still, at your age, your sex partners will probably not have the stamina and control to make sure you always come before they do. So you will have to entice them for a second time, help them to get ready again. Now there are many ways to do this, but the one we going to practice tonight is you being a bit of an exhibitionist for your partner--give him a show to turn him on." He patted the bed next to him. "Come, get in."

Elizabeth began to get up from the floor; but Mr. Shern stopped her.

"No, crawl on your hands and knees. Let me see your tits shake."

Elizabeth lowered herself back down, getting on her hands and knees; and then she began to crawl to her host, moving like a lithe cat, dipping her shoulders in every time she moved so that her breasts swayed heavily below her. When she got to the bed, she climbed on using wide, graceful movements.

"Very good," Mr. Shern nodded. "You are behaving very nicely, Elizabeth. Now, spread your knees, and pull off your panties."

Elizabeth spread her knees on the bed, hooked her fingers into her panties, and pulled them down. But she lowered them slowly, teasing him a bit. Only once they were below the bulging mound of her pussy did she pull them off completely.

Mr. Shern caressed her with his eyes, running them boldly up and down her slim body. Her skin was pale ivory, smooth as cream, and she was breathtaking to behold.

"Play with your breasts," he ordered. She slid her hands up her ribs, cupping her breasts in her palms, pressing and squeezing the soft tissue. As she began to massage her own tits, she tweaked her nipples, pinching them lightly between fingers and gasping out in response.

"Lie down on your back, spread your legs," Mr. Shern said next. Immediately, Elizabeth lowered herself on her elbows, down to her back. Then she opened her knees, letting her host get a good look at her pussy lips. But that wasn't good enough.

"Open your cunt," he said. "Spread your lips open, let me see inside." A bit more hesitantly now, Elizabeth reached in with both hands and pulled her pussy lips apart. Her moist folds stuck together for a second, as if trying to shy away from probing eyes; but exposed to the cool room air, they began to separate, and Mr. Shern drank in the sight of her pink, soft pussy.

Her skin, delicate and fragile, quivered a bit under his gaze. He could see the thick fold of her clitoral hood; beneath it, the swollen button of her blood engorged clitoris peaked out. Her cunt was slightly agape, wet and glistening with her juices, and already it was contracting rhythmically, ready to respond to any stimuli and pull inward.

Mr. Shern could feel his prick begin to expand, and his balls twitch as it did.

"Turn over," he said, his throat dry. "On your hands and knees."

Elizabeth turned over, jutting her ass out toward him. But she kept her legs a bit spread on the bed, so that Mr. Shern could get a good view of her bulging cunt, and he grunted in approval. She was clearly enjoying herself now, and trying her best to give him a good show.

He could still see the worst of the welts where the crop had struck her, but otherwise, her ass was already healing nicely. Just the barest of blushes still spread across her twin cheeks, giving them a rosy glow. He found it enchanting, and all too inviting. He caressed her bottom with his hand, feeling the soft skin, kneading her flesh a bit in a deep, circular motion. Elizabeth moaned.

"Spread your cheeks, let me see your asshole," Mr. Shern said.

Elizabeth froze. No one had ever made such a request of her. It sounded naughty, almost scandalous. *This* would turn him on?

"I'm not going to take you in the ass, Elizabeth," Mr. Shern said gently, his voice full of humor. "I won't even touch you there if it makes you uncomfortable, and clearly it does. We can leave that area for another visit... for now, let me just look."

Elizabeth turned her head around to stare at him. When she saw he was serious, she decided to play along--he had promised only to look--and spread open her cheeks.

And so Mr. Shern was treated to the mouth-watering sight of Elizabeth spreading her ass cheeks apart with delicate hands, revealing before him her virgin asshole. He gazed upon the dark ring of her ass, watching it spasm under his gaze, and felt the blood rush to his engorging cock. Her asshole was a cloudy pink, darker than her cunt, and winked at him charmingly. His cock rose up in response, ready to ram into her delicate tissue.

While she splayed herself out for him on her hands and knees, Mr. Shern positioned himself behind her. Before she knew what he was about, he had lunged into her wet, welcoming cunt.

"Ah!" Elizabeth was thrown forward from the force of his thrust, but he grabbed her by the hips and pulled her back, keeping her in place with his large hands. He began to thrust in and out, ramming her from behind, and Elizabeth closed her eyes and cried out in delight.

His long prick stroked her nerve-filled channel from the inside, rubbing against her exquisitely, and she moaned. She was squeezing against him, contracting her cunt muscles around him without even realizing it, sucking him deeper into her slick pussy until it felt like he was ramming her very womb. And Mr. Shern pounded into her, again and again and again, until Elizabeth was pushed into a mindless state of pure need.

She squeezed her eyes shut and began to make tiny "oh" sounds every time he pounded in, and he drove into her all the way up to his balls, grunting with each thrust.

But after a few luxurious moments, he could feel the first tremors shake her body, and her cunt muscles began to squeeze around him like a vise. He pounded harder, grinding against her ass; and the passionate woman began to thrust back, as if trying to tear her cunt in two with his impaling prick.

"Oh, oh, oh...AHH!" She shook wildly and arched her head up; Mr. Shern pushed her back down and kept ramming her slick hot pussy, enjoying the feel of her tight inner glove spasming against him as she came. She squeezed all around his length, pulling his cock inside.

He came in a flurry of thrusts that would have sent her flying across the bed if he hadn't been holding onto her hips.

In the last moment, she shrieked, another orgasm rising up and overwhelming her senses completely; and then his balls erupted, shooting his sticky cum up her sucking cunt, taking him over the edge for the second time that night.

He waited until his cock was done pulsing his cum inside her, and then he pulled out and fell onto his back across the bed. Elizabeth flattened herself out on her stomach, utterly spent; her muscles were still contracting in tiny aftershocks.

They lay in silence as their breath returned to normal; and then Mr. Shern trailed his hand down her back, tickling her spine, and she shivered.

"You did very well tonight," he said, smiling at her.

"Thank you," she replied softly. They lay in silence a while longer. But the moment soon passed, and he smacked her on the rump.

"Time to get up," he said, going towards his own clothes. Elizabeth took her time getting dressed, then turned to face her host.

"Tomorrow...." she began. Her voice trailed off, and she looked down.

"Tomorrow is your final day," Mr. Shern said. "I expect you here straight after breakfast."

"What....?"

"What will we be doing? I think tomorrow will be a review of sorts. I want to see how far you've come. Literally." He smiled playfully, and Elizabeth blushed.

Three days ago she would have made some flippant response to his comment, tried to show him how worldly she was. Now she looked down demurely, smiling and passing glances at him from the corners of her eyes... Mr. Shern found her absolutely charming, and was quite pleased with her progress.

The liaison arrived, and held open the door for her.

"I will see you tomorrow, Elizabeth. Have a good night."

"Thank you, Sir," she said quietly, and left the room.

*****

The next day, the day of her final activity, Elizabeth was escorted to the same room she and her host had shared for her entire visit (save for her whipping--but she didn't count that). But the room was different now: a large, platform bed took center stage.

Mr. Shern smiled at her when she walked in the room, and Elizabeth felt tears rise up in her eyes. This would be her last visit with Mr. Shern...she was determined to make the most of it.

"Your last day, Elizabeth. Let's not waste a moment. Go ahead and get undressed." The man had an uncanny knack of knowing what she was thinking. Elizabeth grinned and stripped off her clothes. She worked quickly, but kept her eyes on Mr. Shern as she did so, smiling coyly at him when she saw the heat in his eyes.

Once she was naked and standing proudly before him, Mr. Shern ordered her on the bed. Then he went to the wardrobe and returned with a camera.

"What....?" Elizabeth was a little taken aback by the camera. She was under the impression that there would be no lasting evidence of her visit to the Hotel Bentmoore.

"It's an instant camera--no digital copies to be saved, not even by accident. And I'm not keeping the pictures, you are," her host explained. "I thought you might like a little souvenir of your trip, a way to remember all the progress you made here."

Elizabeth looked at the camera with wary eyes, but didn't openly object. As long as she took all the pictures with her, she didn't mind giving it a try.

"Sit up on your knees, and spread them a bit. Arch back, lean on your hands," Mr. Shern instructed. Elizabeth did as told, looking at the camera once she was in place, and heard the distinctive click.

"No go on your stomach and cross your legs behind you--but keep them open a little. Yes, like that. Raise your head up, let your tits fall into the mattress. Perfect." He took another picture.

"Lie on your side, bend your knee just a bit...put a hand on one breast, cup it a bit...now spread your pussy lips so I can see inside."

Elizabeth stopped.

"These pictures are just for you, Elizabeth," Mr. Shern reminded her. "No one else has to see them...but you might want to show them to someone someday." Her host held up the camera and waited.

After a moment, Elizabeth reached down, and with careful fingers, splayed open her vaginal lips, revealing her folds. Mr. Shern took a picture.

"Now up against the bed, and lean over. I want to get a picture between your legs."

Elizabeth moved hesitantly, leaning her torso across the bed as her feet touched the floor. But when she noticed the careful way Mr. Shern was walking, and the enormous pointy bulge in his pants, she relaxed and spread her legs a bit. She was beginning to get turned on, too.

Mr. Shern sat on the floor right by her ankles and held the camera pointed up.

"Spread 'em more," he said, his voice thick. She widened her legs, letting him get the camera all the way up inside, and heard the camera click.

"Now open your cheeks...I want to see it all." Her hands came around to dig into her soft flesh, and she opened her ass for the camera to see. She felt her pussy lips open, too, and widened her legs still further.

"Ahh...yes," Mr. Shern said in approval, and the camera clicked.

He had her pose in different positions all over the room, and when he was done, dozens of instant pictures lay scattered across the floor. Then Mr. Shern quickly undressed and joined her on the bed, falling between her splayed legs. He began to suck on her tits, pulling the hardened nipples into his mouth, and Elizabeth arched into him.

A second later he was ramming his swollen cock right up her wet cunt, and the highly aroused woman wrapped her arms around him, pulling him into her. When that wasn't enough she grabbed him by the ass, trying to push him in even deeper, and ground her pelvis against him. Her cunt squeezed, and her clitoris throbbed...She made little keening noises every time he moved.

He leaned back on his knees until only the head of his cock was still lodged up her cunt, and then he raised her legs up by her ankles. Now when he thrust in, he could go in harder and deeper than before, and it felt to Elizabeth like he was trying to ram her all the way up her body. She arched and cried out in ecstasy, grabbing fistfuls of the sheet in both hands and squeezing her eyes tight.

"Don't come yet," Mr. Shern growled, and began to thrust harder. Elizabeth began to make a series of tiny "oh" sounds, trying to hang on. Her pelvic muscles tensed and constricted, and her pussy squeezed around his plunging prick.

"Not yet, Elizabeth," he ordered again; he raised her legs higher. Elizabeth cried out and writhed on the bed. She could feel her legs trembling in his strong hands. It felt so good, *so good....*

"Now," Mr. Shern said, and Elizabeth came, an explosion that began inside her liquid hot pussy and radiated out the rest of her body. It didn't end for a long time, but went on, like exploding firecrackers of bliss, and when Elizabeth felt Mr. Shern's cock inside her stiffen even more before he, too, erupted, she came again, gripping her cunt tissues around his hard length like she was trying to swallow him up inside.

But at last, when they were both done, and Mr. Shern fell across her sweaty, heaving body, Elizabeth grinned and kissed him lightly on the shoulder.

"That was good," her host said, grinning back at her. "I'll give you a few minutes to rest before we start again." Elizabeth's eyes went wide, and then she smiled in delight.

He had her come twice more before their time was up. By the time Elizabeth was ordered to get dressed, she was walking rather stiffly, and somewhat bow-legged. But she didn't notice...at least, she didn't seem to care.

Mr. Shern gathered up the pictures, slid them into a square black envelope, and handed the package over to Elizabeth.

"Here you go," he said. "Your memento."

Elizabeth opened the envelope and pulled one out: it was a photo of her on the bed, pinching both her nipples, looking up at the camera seductively.

"I want you to have this," she said quietly. "Just... promise me you won't show anyone."

"I won't," Mr. Shern promised. "I'll keep it safe. And thank you, Elizabeth."

"Thank you, Sir," she replied, and looked down sadly. She felt like she was about to cry. "I...I can come back though, right?"

"You can come back to the Hotel Bentmoore when-ever you want. And you can request me as your host, too--although I would suggest you try some of the other hosts, as well. We all have our own strengths and talents. You might enjoy Mr. Sinclaire, the man you met yesterday, for instance."

"Thank you Sir," she said, and smiled. She could come back whenever she wanted, and continue on this path she had started...she could even experiment with a different host...but she would always remember Mr. Shern, her first host, in a special way.

*****

When her stepmother arrived to pick her up at the front of the hotel, Elizabeth slid her suitcase into the trunk of the car and ran around to the passenger seat. As her stepmother drove, Elizabeth watched out the window as the hotel soon disappeared from view.

"So? How was it?"

"It was...good," Elizabeth said. Her stepmother passed her glances as she drove, noticing already the subtle changes within the young woman.

Elizabeth was no longer tense, on edge, and slightly angry at the world. She was calmer now, more at ease within herself, like she could stand to be in her own skin.

"Good," the older woman said, nodding in satisfaction. But Elizabeth surprised her even further.

"Thank you, Stepmama, for bringing me here," she said quietly. "I...I needed it."

"You're welcome, Elizabeth," she said softly, feeling a world of difference from her stepdaughter. Things were going to be different now, she knew. She smiled.

She would remain at home for a few weeks, help Elizabeth's father get used to this new daughter of his, help Elizabeth ease back into her life and start to make some plans for her future.

And then...then Elizabeth's stepmother would be taking her own little vacation.

Her room at the Hotel Bentmoore had already been reserved.

Also by Shelby Cross

Short stories:

Masters of the Hotel Bentmoore: Michelle
Masters of the Hotel Bentmoore: Samantha
Masters of the Hotel Bentmoore: Evie
Masters of the Hotel Bentmoore: Khloe

Compilation:

Masters of the Hotel Bentmoore: The Complete Series

Coming Soon:

The Taming of Red Riding
The Edge of Jasmine